VEGAS
VENGEANCE

VEGAS VENGEANCE

RANDY WAYNE
WHITE
WRITING AS CARL RAMM

OPEN ROAD

INTEGRATED MEDIA

NEW YORK

Cover design by Andy Ross

ISBN: 978-1-5040-3519-4

This edition published in 2016 by Open Road Integrated Media, Inc.
180 Maiden Lane
New York, NY 10038
www.openroadmedia.com

VEGAS
VENGEANCE

ONE

James Hawker found her in the Yellow Pages.

Under prostitution.

A four by four ad in the hotel directory sandwiched with a dozen others between Process Servers and Psychologists.

It seemed appropriate that the three headings should fall into such a convenient order.

The ad affected an Elizabethan motif: drawing of a plump lady on a plush couch beneath an ornate chandelier:

The Doll House.
A reputable house for the discriminating gentleman.

There were two telephone numbers in bold print, along with an address. Beneath, in light script, was the reminder:

It's Legal in Las Vegas.

Hawker almost smiled. When had anything ever been illegal in Las Vegas? It was a wide-open town. Always had been. Always would be.

Even long before the white man came to Vegas, the local Paiute Indians were said to have been addicted to gambling. They rolled human bones in the sand and bet their wives and favorite horses. Then came the days of the gold and silver rush, and Las Vegas became a mining town. Poker debts and whores were paid for with raw gold nuggets.

After the gold and silver ran out, Nevada seemed to be left with only one natural resource: the freewheeling attitude of its citizenry. In 1931, the state legislature legalized gambling. But the clientele was mostly local, mostly ranch hands and construction workers.

Then, in 1955, a Mormon banker named E. Parry Thomas came to town and realized that while gambling fever was not unique, a municipality that would tolerate it in the open was. Las Vegas, he decided, had something very special to offer the world. Thomas risked huge loans to back the construction of gambling palaces.

Modern-day Las Vegas was born.

So Las Vegas had always been a wide-open town. It was, in fact, only within the last twenty years that a gambler could go there and be sure that if he played the legitimate houses, he would be given a straight deal.

Everything was legal in Las Vegas. And the prim establishment loved it. An ultraconservative businessman from, say, Des Moines could leave his wife, kids and life of respectability behind and spend a weekend in Vegas whoring, drinking, gambling, indulging his every whim or perversion at great expense—but in relative safety.

Las Vegas was the blossom of America's dark fantasy. A small desert town, population less than. 200,000; that was open 24 hours a day, 365 days a year. A small desert town built on sand dunes and rimmed by blue mountains; a town that, at night, sent a gaudy, blazing neon flame brighter than Broadway's into the Nevada darkness.

A wide-open town. Gambling. Prostitution. Fast marriages, faster divorces. Booze and drugs.

But lately, it was even more wide open than usual.

Murder had been added to the city's list of vices.

Murder and extortion.

James Hawker closed the directory and picked up the phone. While he waited for an outside line, he surveyed his hotel room closely for the first time.

Kevin Smith had given him one of the best his gambling complex, the Mirage, had to offer.

A two-bedroom suite done in pale blues and desert grays.

There were copies of good watercolors and oils on the walls by Western artists: haunting landscapes of buttes and plains; raw-faced cowboys riding herd.

There was a sunken living room with ankle-deep pile carpet and a spa-size bathroom complete with whirlpool bath and mirrored walls. The balcony overlooked the Olympic-size swimming pool in the middle of the complex, and Hawker carried the phone out onto the balcony.

It was 11 A.M., and the showgirls were spending their off hours in the sun.

They lay beneath him on lounge chairs, an oiled row of lithe legs and heavy breasts in candy-colored bikinis. Blondes, brunettes and redheads sipping at drinks and rubbing on lotion.

Hawker dialed the number.

"The Doll House. Can we please you in some way?"

The girl who answered had a husky, sensual voice edged with just a hint of teenybopper.

"My name is Hawker. I'd like to speak with Barbara Blaine."

The girl hesitated. "If you're interested in setting up a private party, I can do that for you."

"I'm not interested in a private party."

"Then you know that Ms. Blaine isn't . . . she employs the other girls who work here. She owns the business."

Hawker smiled. "I know Ms. Blaine isn't for hire, if that's what you mean. And I would still like to speak with her."

"Hang on then, Mr. Hawker. I'll see if she's in."

"Tell her I'm a friend of Kevin Smith's."

The girl brightened. "Captain Smith? Yes, Mr. Hawker, of course I will."

There was nothing overtly sensual in the voice of Barbara Blaine. It was a cool alto with the controlled friendliness businesspeople reserve for the acquaintances of friends.

"Yes, Mr. Hawker. How can I help you?"

Below the balcony, one of the showgirls stood. A leggy woman in her early twenties with a rich mane of auburn hair, she wore a bright lime bikini, and she had forgotten that she had untied the top. It slipped down off her breasts, showing the wide pink areolas and upturned nipples. Unflustered, she calmly tied the bikini top back on, laughed at something the other girls called out to her, then dove headlong into the Jell-O-blue water of the pool.

Just before she went in, she glanced up and saw Hawker watching her.

When she saw that Hawker was not embarrassed, she grinned. There was something in her open, handsome face that reminded Hawker of someone.

A girl from not so long ago.

A girl he had loved. A girl whom he had lost to a bullet. A girl named Megan.

Hawker looked away from the pool, clearing his throat. "I'm a friend of Kevin Smith's, Ms. Blaine," he said. "Kevin told me about the trouble he and the other casino owners in the Five-Cs complex are having. He also suggested that your business was having the same kind of trouble."

"Yes?" Her voice had turned cool.

"Kevin asked me to check into it. I'd like to help him if I can—and you, too. Could we get together and talk?"

"Are you a cop, Mr. Hawker?"

"No."

"A private investigator?"

"In a way. Yes."

"It's just that I find it odd that Captain Smith and his associates would find it necessary to bring in outside . . . help. After all, Captain Smith and Captain Wells and Mr. Kullenburg and the others are all ex-Vegas policemen. Thus the name of the complex: the Five-Cs. The five cops."

"You're welcome to call Captain Smith if you have any doubts, Ms. Blaine. He said you would probably insist on it. He said you're a hard-nosed businesswoman who doesn't take any chances."

Hawker could sense the woman smiling at the other end of the line. "Did he now? And what else did he say?"

7

"He told me that your lover of two years, Jason Stratton, disappeared three weeks ago and you think he's been murdered."

"I don't *think* he's been murdered, Mr. Hawker. I know he's been murdered."

"Then you have proof?"

"None that the official police will listen to. But we can talk about that privately, Mr. Hawker. Say in an hour? At my office?"

"I was thinking dinner might be better, Ms. Blaine. Seven in the Von Hoff Room?"

"Going to spend the day looking for clues, Mr. Hawker?"

"Kevin also said you had a gift for sarcasm. And I am going to look for leads, as a matter of fact. I'm going to drive to Mr. Stratton's cabin and have a look around."

"You won't find anything. The police didn't—and it's thirty miles from downtown Vegas."

"Kevin told me how to get there."

"The stubborn type, huh? Okay, then dinner it is, Mr. Hawker—if Captain Smith *does* confirm that you're working for him."

"I'll see you then—"

"Mr. Hawker," the woman cut in, "I'm sure Captain Smith has already warned you, but let me warn you again. The people who want to take over the Five-Cs complex and my business will stop at nothing. They would have murdered us long ago if the resulting publicity wouldn't make it impossible for them to consummate the takeover without a federal investigation. But Jason Stratton was an outsider. That's why they killed him. It was a way of pressuring me. And you're an outsider, Mr. Hawker.

They'll kill you the moment they find out you're nosing around. Remember that."

"And why do you think they want your business so badly, Ms. Blaine?"

James Hawker repeated the question once more before he realized the woman had already hung up.

TWO

Hawker checked the suite's refrigerator before stripping off his clothes.

Kevin Smith had had his people load it with bottled beer and gourmet sandwich fixings.

On the chauffeured ride from the airport, Smith had warned him about the bad room service—an odd thing for the president of a hotel syndicate to do. But when he explained why, it made sense.

"You've got to first understand that Vegas is legit, James. Mostly legit," Smith had said. He was a barrel-chested man who still looked more like a cop than a casino manager.

"Why risk the license of a multimillion-dollar gambling plant just to cheat a customer out of a few thousand? See? Cheating doesn't make sense. If we can get our customers to gamble, then we win, because the odds are in our favor. It's a matter of mathematics. The house has just under a two percent edge in craps and blackjack, about a six percent edge in roulette, a ten percent edge with slot machines and a twenty percent edge in keno. For every one person who leaves Vegas a big winner, there are eighty others flying out losers. The other nineteen percent maybe win a little or break even. You see, cheating is stupid because we're going to win anyway—as long as we get our guests to the gambling tables."

Hawker had listened carefully—not because he was interested in gambling. He wasn't. But he knew he had to familiarize himself with the philosophy of the Vegas business establishment in order to crack the mob that was now using murder and extortion to chase Kevin Smith and his associates out of the Five-Cs complex.

"Getting people to gamble is the key," Smith had continued. "And to do that, we use tricks. We offer deluxe rooms and gourmet food at less than break-even prices. That gets them to Vegas, but it doesn't get them into our casinos. So we make the food in the restaurant just as good as we can get it—and make room service bad enough so our customers will *have* to go to the restaurant. The plant is designed so they have to walk through the casino to get to the restaurant. See? Same with the floor shows. We run a heavy entertainment nut, but the tables give it all back to us. We book big-name stars. Nothing but the best: Sinatra, Ann-Margret, Johnny Carson. We make the tickets cheap, and we hand out plenty of comps to people we know to be heavy gamblers. But they have to walk through the casino to get to the show. Smart, huh?

"Once they're in the casino, of course, our people take very damn good care of them. Free drinks, free food and perfect service. And that's a trick, too. We figure it costs us more for a gambler to be away from the table buying a drink than it does for us to give the gambler that drink free. See what I mean? It's all legit, but it's a trick. That's why you shouldn't expect much from room service, Hawk. Even if I gave my room service people direct orders to take care of you, they'd still be sloppy because that's the kind of people I have to have working in room service."

So Hawker was glad for the refrigerator—and amused by Vegas economics.

Hawker opened a frosted bottle of Tuborg, turned the whirlpool bath on high and settled himself into the 120-degree water.

He'd flown in from Chicago that morning, with four sour flight attendants and a capacity load of revelers all energized by booze and the hope of beating the tables of Vegas.

They wouldn't, of course. Like Kevin Smith said, it was a question of mathematics.

He had spent about an hour with Smith on a short tour of the hotel. But mostly Smith had talked about the goons who were trying to force him out of business.

He didn't have to tell him much.

Hawker's own friend and associate Jacob Montgomery Hayes had told him enough for him to know it was another job that couldn't be handled effectively by the official police.

It was a job that called for a vigilante. Someone who could move on the shadowy outskirts of the law. Someone who could move quickly and decisively. Someone who wasn't afraid to kill—or be killed.

Hawker finished his whirlpool, wrapped the towel around his waist and went to the balcony.

The showgirl with the thick auburn hair and long legs was gone.

Hawker was surprised at the disappointment he felt.

He liked women. He liked the smell of them, the feel of them, the deep throaty sounds they made in the ecstasy of bed.

But he had felt true emotion for very few of them. Hawker was honest enough with himself to admit that he used women for the pleasure they could provide him—just as the women he had been with used him.

There was seldom anything more than that. Women were a pleasurable necessity. Like fresh air.

Hawker turned from the balcony and went back into the canned chill of his room.

After unpacking, he dressed himself in gray cavalry twill slacks, a pale blue Royal Oxford shirt, a pair of glove-soft lamb's wool socks, then pulled on a cobalt doeskin flannel blazer.

In Las Vegas, a city of mobility and temporary relationships, Hawker knew first impressions were more important than in most places. He wanted to look moneyed without looking flashy. Once again he surprised himself as he realized that he really *was* wealthy. Not a millionaire. Not yet. But there was more money socked away in his Chicago account and his New Cayman Island account than he had ever dreamed of.

On his last assignment, he had become a partner in a south Texas oil company. Vice-president, in fact. His partners in the company knew nothing about drilling for oil. But they had something better going for them. They were lucky. Very damn lucky. And now they were all wealthy men.

Hawker thought it funny that he had found almost no use for the money. He cared little for the stuff. The one purchase he had made was that of a house on the wilderness southwest coast of Florida. A cypress house built on stilts on a broad tidal river.

13

He had yet to see the house.

But he liked the idea of having a place to go when he wanted to get away and fish or just be alone.

He had given a fair share of the money to friends as loans or outright gifts. That which was left over went into the bank accounts.

He sometimes wondered if he would live long enough to find a use for all the money.

When Hawker was finished dressing, he went into the suite's second bedroom. Jacob Montgomery Hayes had shipped his arsenal of equipment in wooden crates—by private courier, of course.

Hawker opened one of the crates and selected the two weapons he would never be without on this assignment.

The first was his Randall Model 18 Attack/Survival knife, made especially for Hawker by Bo Randall's craftsmen in Orlando, Florida. Hawker had used the Randall in more than one very tough spot, and he had full confidence in the weapon's integrity. He pulled up a slacks leg, strapped the custom-built scabbard over his calf-high sock and inserted the heavy knife.

The second weapon was a Walther PPK automatic. The Walther was small enough to wear unobtrusively in the spring-loaded shoulder holster beneath his sport coat. Yet, in nine millimeter, it had enough firepower with its eight-round detachable clip to be a solid man-stopper. The Walther had the expected drawbacks of every automatic handgun: it lacked killing range and accuracy, and there was always the chance it would jam.

But, as James Hawker knew better than most, every firearm

was a compromise. The trick was to match the strengths of the weaponry to the demands of the assignment.

And this Las Vegas encounter, he knew, had to be a low-profile operation. He had to be able to blend into the gambling scene unnoticed, yet be able to sting the mob when the opportunity presented itself.

In Hawker's mind, keeping a low profile meant leaving no bodies for the police to find.

THREE

Hawker took the elevator down and stepped out into the casino hallway of the Mirage Hotel.

The hall was done in plush burgundy carpet and coppery velvet wallpaper.

The decor was suggestive of a San Francisco beer hall during the gold-rush days of the late 1800s. The furnishings were done in rich mahogany and polished brass.

Kevin Smith had explained the setup to him. There were five casinos in the Five-Cs complex. Each of the five ex-cops involved had invested his life savings to found a syndicate to build this small gambling center on the outskirts of downtown Vegas, east of the famous Vegas strip.

The plot of land they had developed was a twenty-acre wedge of sand and rank weed near nothing but a fast four-lane, Highway 95. The five cops had their own ideas about what Vegas casinos could be and they wanted their business separated from the famous Las Vegas both spiritually and physically. They had used the purchase of the land both as collateral and as a sign of their good faith. On that commitment, they had borrowed enough money to begin their syndicate.

They were well known in Vegas, well liked and trusted. They had no trouble getting backers. They built the five casinos in a semi-circle, with Captain Smith's, the largest, in the middle.

The Mirage.

But this casino was no mirage. It was a dream that had come true.

Each of the five casinos was different, reflective of the idiosyncratic personalities of the detectives who were the principal owners.

Kevin Smith was an Old West buff. Read all of Zane Grey. Collected antique weaponry. Liked the idea of his showgirls wearing heavy petticoats, dresses of scarlet satin and billowing plume hats. His casino emphasized the elegance of that era— particularly the feminine kind. Captain Smith had hired the most beautiful women in Vegas to dance the floor shows and work the casino.

One of the other cops was an outdoorsman. Liked hunting and fishing. He decorated his casino like an elite men's club: plush leather furniture, gigantic stone fireplaces, mounted tarpon and elk on the walls.

The other casinos were equally individualized. As a result, they seemed to attract a better and more loyal clientele.

As Hawker stepped into the hallway, he noted that there were times when even clientele of the highest class looked bad.

It was a Friday morning, but the haggard faces of the men and women in the casino said it was very late Thursday night.

In the casino, full-breasted waitresses in tight shorts and

cowboy hats carried drinks on trays to the men and women hunched over the craps and blackjack tables. The casino's piped-in music was fast and jazzy.

There were no clocks on any of the walls.

In the front hall, a couple of dozen matronly women kept the slot machines busy. Bells clanked, lights flashed and the machines whirred. The women played with a religious intensity, stopping only to light cigarettes or get more change.

Hawker wondered how many of them knew that of the two billion dollars in winnings the Vegas casinos took in annually, the largest percentage of the money came not from the glamour games—blackjack and roulette—but from slot machines.

The billion-dollar shimmer of Vegas was fired by the nickels and quarters of America's matriarchs.

Straightening his tie, Hawker made his way down the hall to the front desk.

The desk was mahogany and brass. Behind it was a switchboard and two personal computer stations for handling reservations. Hawker jotted a note telling Kevin Smith his plans for the afternoon and asked the deskman for an envelope.

"You'll give this to Mr. Smith?"

The deskman's nod was as European as his accent. "Of course, Mr. Hawker. I'll deliver it personally. Is there anything else I can do for you?"

"Captain Smith said something about a car being at my disposal."

"Anything you wish, Mr. Hawker. Those were our instructions." The deskman allowed himself a sophisticated pause that seemed to be the equivalent of a smile. "Cars, food, chips for the casino . . . women—or whatever diversion you choose." He shrugged humorously. "Of course, I can't provide you with a woman from the casino. Mr. Smith doesn't approve of that sort of thing and doesn't allow it—"

"I'll settle for just a car right now."

"Would you like a car with a driver? Perhaps a nice tour of the city?"

"No. Just a car. And a map."

"Of Las Vegas?"

"Of Nevada."

"Ah!" There was the implication of a smile again. "I think we have just the vehicle for a day of touring." He tapped the brass bell sharply. The bellboy wore the red double-breasted jacket and round red hat of a bellboy from the old days.

The deskman held out a set of keys. "Bring number six around from the casino car pool for Mr. Hawker. Make sure it's fueled and ready for a long drive." He looked at Hawker. "Can we have the kitchen pack a lunch for you? Perhaps some cracked crab and a split of champagne on ice?"

"A car," said Hawker, growing impatient. "All I want is a car."

The deskman nodded at the bellboy. "You heard Mr. Hawker. A car right away!"

Hawker followed the bellboy outside and waited on the curb. The valets were men in their early twenties. They wore white dinner jackets. Hawker wondered how they kept from looking bored. He guessed it was because Captain Smith had ordered them not to.

Smith ran a tight ship. No doubt about that.

When the bellboy finally came with the car, Hawker did a double take.

"Are you sure that's the car I'm supposed to use?"

The bellboy grinned. "This is the one. Number six." He held out the keys. "Some machine, huh, Mr. Hawker? Some French count or someone like that transferred the title to Mr. Smith to settle a gambling debt."

"A gambling debt? How much did he lose?"

"I heard about twenty grand. I guess the car would be worth more than that, huh?"

Hawker ran his hand over the fender. It was a vintage twelve-cylinder Jaguar XKE convertible. Maybe a 1961 or '62. Midnight blue with light blue leather interior, all in absolutely mint condition.

"More," said Hawker. "Considerably more, I would guess."

"When Mr. Smith first took it in trade, he had a mechanic make sure it was in tip-top shape. Engine, brakes, tires, everything. Then he took it out on the flats to see what she would do. He never really said how fast he got her up to, but I saw him when he got back. His face looked kind of pale and his hands were shaking." The bellboy laughed. "My guess was that he quit before this baby did. I'd say a hundred and sixty would be conservative. Gas was cheap back then, and they built 'em fast."

Hawker slid in behind the walnut veneer and the bank of gauges.

The convertible canvas was down and the car smelled of fresh leather.

He shifted into first and touched the accelerator. The bank of mufflers burbled huskily as he drove out of the parking lot, around the circle that connected the five casinos and onto the main road.

It was a spring day in Nevada. High, clear sky of the palest blue. A dry wind blew across the sand flats, cooled by the distant mountains of Toiyabe Range.

The wind whipped through Hawker's dark red-brown hair as he drove. Once he was on the open road, he had to suppress the adolescent urge to flatten the accelerator and see just how fast the Jag really would go.

Instead, he kept it at a comfortable sixty-five.

There was too much on his mind to concentrate on high-speed driving.

Kevin Smith had told him a little about the problems they had been having. There had been telephone threats. Some careful vandalism. One of his associates, Charlie Kullenburg, had been beaten almost to death. And Barbara Blaine's boyfriend had disappeared.

Hawker had pressed for all Smith knew about Jason Stratton, the young man who, in Barbara Blaine's opinion, had been murdered.

Stratton was an outsider. Something of a hermit. Lived in a mountain cabin on a secondary road that led to Kyle Canyon. Liked classical music, good books and intelligent talk. Stratton pieced together a livelihood by operating a backroom biological specimens wholesale business.

He collected insects, snakes, fossils and sold them to the universities.

Stratton also made a little money as a watercolor artist and as a pulp fiction writer.

It was an odd love affair: an intellectual recluse and the proprietor of a whorehouse.

Hawker doubted there was anything to gain by visiting Stratton's cottage. The local cops had already gone over it—but not as carefully as they probably would have if there'd been a corpse involved.

Stratton had been listed as a missing person.

In Las Vegas, people turned up missing every day of the year. Usually by choice.

So Hawker doubted if the cops had given the place a thorough search. At least he hoped they hadn't, because it was really the only thing he had to go on.

At State Route 157, he turned southwest, then left again onto a dirt road. According to Captain Smith's directions, Jason Stratton's cabin wasn't far.

The mountains were ahead of him now, cool and smoky blue in the distance. He had passed no cars for some time, so he noticed immediately when the black Datsun 280Z came charging out behind him, blasting a plume of red dust.

The Datsun surged right up behind him, disappearing in the dust wake of Hawker's Jag.

Hawker backed off on the accelerator, figuring it was some teenager who wanted to race. Some acne-faced kid who, like too many adult male drivers, used the gearshift as an extension of his libido.

He expected the Datsun to pass, but it didn't. Instead, it edged right up behind and nudged the Jag's bumper.

Hawker's face tightened and he swore softly. He glanced at the speedometer. He had slowed to forty-five. Even at that speed, the nudge on the bumper caused him to fishtail slightly.

He slowed even more, pulling off the dirt road to the right a little to give the Datsun one more chance to pass.

Instead, it smacked him in the rear bumper again.

Hawker knew then. He knew it was no teenager out for a joyride. He knew that somehow the mob had found out about his arrival, and about his plans to search Jason Stratton's cabin.

This was no childish encounter on a mountain road. This was an assassination attempt. A matter of life and death.

Calmly Hawker reached beneath his jacket and placed the Walther PPK in the bucket seat beside him. He glanced over his shoulder to see how many men were in the Datsun, but the dust squall thrown by the Jag made it impossible to tell.

Once again the Datsun rammed him, and Hawker had to fight to keep the British sports car on the road.

Somehow he had to get behind them. Or beside them. But first, he had to get ahead of them. Way ahead of them.

Then, if he could, he would find some way to get them out of their car and force information out of them.

Information was what he needed now. Not corpses.

The corpses would come later.

FOUR

James Hawker downshifted into second and put the Jag into a controlled drift to make a solid dust screen across the road. Then he straightened the car on the weedy shoulder, where traction would be best, and accelerated.

Hawker was no stranger to high-performance automobiles. He owned a classic Corvette fastback, a gem he had rescued from the police auction table and had refurbished by a master mechanic friend of his, Big Nick Clements.

But even the Vet didn't compare to this XKE for sheer power and handling ability.

When he touched the accelerator, the Jag seemed to flatten itself over the road as the tires struggled for purchase. When the treads caught, the car lunged forward at a velocity beyond Hawker's imagination. The G-force pinned his head to the neck brace.

Holding the steering wheel at the ten and two position, he glanced at the speedometer when he was sure he had the vehicle under control.

He had gone from forty to ninety miles an hour in a matter of only a few seconds.

He checked the rearview mirror.

The 280Z was a hundred yards behind, but gaining on him.

The dirt road was narrow but relatively smooth. Hawker was grateful for that. At high speed, a single pothole could prove fatal. He concentrated on reading the road, his left foot riding lightly midway between the brake and the clutch.

Hawker was aware that the road was climbing steadily. These would be the foothills near Kyle Canyon. Off to his left, he saw a small brown cabin near a river flash past. He wondered if it was Jason Stratton's cabin.

But he didn't have long to think about it. Ahead, the yellow road sign told him he was about to enter a series of hairpin curves.

The bank of mufflers roared as he downshifted into third, then second. The Jag skidded and held as he accelerated his way through the S turns.

Off to his left now was the beginning of the canyon. A short piece of corrugated guardrail was all that separated the road from the sheer drop to the rocks below. Three white wooden crosses were planted near the rail; people had died here before.

Coming out of the hairpin curves, Hawker mashed the accelerator flat and held it on the long straightaway until the speedometer hit 130 miles an hour.

The road was asphalt here, and the Jag seemed to absorb the white dividing lines ahead. Trees and telephone poles streamed past in a blur. Beyond the straightaway, Hawker could see that the road ribboned its way up the mountain.

He swore softly.

Somewhere there had to be a turnoff. Some place he could lose his attackers and reappear behind them.

The Datsun was about seventy yards behind now and no longer gaining. Without the dust haze, he could see that there were at least two people in the car. Two men.

The next bank of curves appeared with less warning. But at 130 miles an hour, everything happens with less warning.

Hawker touched the brake the moment he saw the yellow sign and prepared to downshift. His concentration was broken momentarily when a rock apparently flew up, shattering the Jag's windshield.

But then he realized it was no rock.

It was a bullet.

A man was leaning out the window of the 280Z. A man with a rifle.

Hawker knew it would take a phenomenally lucky shot to hit him at that distance from a moving car.

Even so, it didn't make driving any easier.

Now more than ever he had to put distance between the two cars and find a turnoff, a place he could lose them.

But first, he had to make it off this road alive.

Hawker hit the curves faster than he wanted to. He downshifted, braked—and was fully prepared for the Jag to flip and begin the long and deadly slow-motion tumble down the mountain.

But the Jag handled as if bolted to rails. The tires screamed briefly as he drifted through the first curve, then held fast as he accelerated into the next swing to the left.

Another right bank, then a swing left, another curve to the right, and he was working the Jaguar through the gears again, powering hard down the straightaway.

There was no warning for what happened next. Highway departments do not post warning signs for hills. Only yellow no-passing lines.

As Hawker came to the top of the hill, he found himself slowing slightly through sheer habit. Only fools top a hill without slowing, for there is no telling what is on the other side—a car stalled, some idiot passing. Hawker had been a cop too long and seen too many lives wasted through sheer carelessness and childish bravado not to have good driving habits.

And it was the little bit he slowed that saved him.

As he topped the hill, he immediately saw the man with the flag. An old man in coveralls waving a red towel on a stick.

The old man was driving a herd of sheep from one pasture to the next, his black-haired collie nipping at the heels of the animals; a flock of a couple of hundred.

At the bottom of the hill was a curve. A guardrail cupped the asphalt from the rocky gorge below. To the right was a low rock ledge, on top of which was a pasture fenced by wire paling. The sheep covered both lanes of the road, with the old man trailing behind.

Hawker hit the brakes immediately, but with controlled pressure so the wheels did not lock. The old man was waving his arms over his head frantically. The collie paid no heed, tending to the business of guiding the sheep.

It was the dog that gave Hawker his opening. It cut outside the herd, and the sheep flushed toward the right lane. It was a small opening, but Hawker had no choice. The old man was directly in his path now.

He downshifted, hit the accelerator and the Jag jumped through the narrow opening between the dog and the guardrail, throwing gravel.

The opening widened momentarily after he passed, then closed again.

Hawker was on a straightaway now, and he watched through the rearview mirror to see how the driver of the 280Z handled the roadblock.

The Datsun topped the hill at such tremendous speed that all four wheels temporarily left the asphalt. When the car touched down again, the driver appeared to brake briefly and downshift—but too late.

The 280Z hit the herd of sheep going about forty. Hawker saw the old man sag slightly as the collie was knocked high in the air, somersaulting like a rag animal. The car skidded left, then right, leaving a wake of screaming, kicking sheep behind.

The driver of the car brought the 280Z under control again, accelerating toward Hawker. Then Hawker was into the next curve and he could see no more.

It had been a sickening thing to witness, and Hawker sped on grimly.

Ahead was another straightaway climbing toward another hill. He was well into the mountains now, more than two miles above sea level. Below were the moonscape crags of the canyon.

Hawker held the accelerator to the floor, and the speedometer touched 155 before he backed off for the hill. He was about a quarter-mile ahead of the Datsun now. It was all the room he needed to make a move.

At the top of the hill, he slowed to sixty. An eighth of a mile down the hill, he hit the brakes and stopped the Jag in a controlled skid. To the right was a dirt lane that climbed back into the mountains. It was a blind intersection, shielded by a high rock ledge.

It was just what Hawker was looking for.

He punched the Jaguar into reverse and backed into the lane far enough so that he was hidden from anyone passing on the main road. It was his plan to come out behind the Datsun, force it off the road, then beat some information out of the two goons inside.

But then he had another idea.

Hawker edged the car back onto the main road, blocking both lanes. In front of him was a guardrail and a sheer five-hundred-foot drop onto the rocks below. Behind him was the dirt trail.

Hawker shifted the Jag into reverse and waited.

The driver of the 280Z hadn't learned anything from his disaster with the sheep. He flew over the hill at full speed. Hawker wondered what was going through the driver's mind as he saw the Jag blocking his path less than two hundred yards away.

The Datsun skidded wildly, fishtailing down the hill. Hawker waited until the last possible moment before gunning the Jag backward, out of harm's way.

It was too late to help the men in the 280Z.

The driver of the Datsun made the wisest possible choice.

Rather than broadside the Jag or go over the cliff, he slowed his car by careening along the stone ledge on the inside edge of the road.

There was the nauseating scream of wrenching metal. A rocky outcrop caught the right bumper, spinning the car in a violent 360-degree turn. Then the Datsun flipped side over side, tumbling three times before finally coming to rest on its wheels just past the dirt lane.

Hawker grabbed the Walther PPK and trotted to the wrecked 280Z. One of the men was already climbing out through the shattered front window.

Hawker expected him to get dizzily to his feet, hands held high in surrender.

He didn't.

He was a lanky man with dark curly hair worn down to his shoulders. The yellow leisure suit didn't go with the face: thin, angular, ratlike. He got out from the passenger's side. He was the man who had been shooting at Hawker.

But he carried no rifle now.

He took two wobbly steps toward Hawker, his hands held low. "Does your car still run?" the man asked groggily.

"Yeah. But some asshole shot out the window."

"That's good. We'll have transportation."

Hawker thought it was an odd thing to say until the stainless-steel stubnose .38 materialized in the man's right hand, lifting toward Hawker's face.

Hawker was so taken by surprise that the only thing he could do was drop backward to the ground.

The gunshot and the vacuum Hawker felt near his head were simultaneous.

Hawker rolled hard to his left and came up firing. The little Walther snapped twice in his hand.

The man in the yellow leisure suit twisted sideways, his face contorted in shock and pain. There were two red pockmarks on the lapel of the suit. The left lapel. Then the pockmarks became soggy black stains, and the man fell dead, clutching his chest.

In the sudden silence, Hawker could hear the steady hiss of steam coming from the wrecked Datsun and the trickle of liquid. And something else, too. A low moan. A man's voice:

"Hey? Hey! Louie! You out there? Get me the hell out of here, for God's sake!"

Hawker walked around to the driver's side of the 280Z. The driver looked to be in his early thirties. He was stockier than the other man, Louie. Heavy, swarthy face. Blue shadow of beard. A cut on his forehead dripped blood down over his left eye. Even so, both eyes grew wide when he looked up and saw Hawker.

"Hey! Where's my partner? Where's Louie?"

Hawker brought the Walther into view as if in explanation. "Dead."

"You killed him?"

"Indirectly. He pulled a gun on me."

"What's that supposed to mean?"

"It means your buddy committed suicide. By proxy."

The man's hand shook as he wiped the blood from his face. "Hey, you're not going to kill me, are you? I'm hurt. Hurt bad. My legs are pinned under this damn steering wheel, and I think they're broke. Both of 'em."

"You expect me to feel sorry for you?"

The man reached one hand out toward Hawker, pleading.

31

"Look, buddy, it was nothing personal. We get paid to carry out orders. You were nothing but a job. No sense in getting personal about it."

"Who gave you the orders?"

"Hell, buddy, I can't tell you that!"

Hawker bounced the Walther in his hand. "You don't have much choice—*buddy.*"

The man strained to pull himself from beneath the steering wheel and grimaced with pain. He wiped more blood from his face, then looked at Hawker. "Okay, okay, I'll talk. But first you got to get me out of here. This hurts too bad. I can't even think straight."

"You can think straight enough for what I need to know. First you talk. Then I get you out."

"You bastard!" the man snarled. "I might be bleeding to death!"

"All the more reason to hurry, friend."

The man nodded quickly. "Okay, I'll tell you what I know. But it isn't much, honest to god. Christ, if they ever found out I talked, they'd—they'd—"

"They'd do just what I plan to do if you don't talk," Hawker cut in. "With them, at least you have a chance. Tell them you had a wreck chasing me. Tell them I got away. No way they can find out you talked. Your buddy sure as hell isn't going to tell them."

The worry on the man's face wasn't contrived. "You don't know those animals. Hell, I'd rather have a bullet through the brain than what they'd do to me."

Hawker lifted the automatic. "I'll be happy to oblige if that's what you want."

VEGAS VENGEANCE

The man held his palms toward him. "Not so quick, for Christ's sake. I told you I'd talk. What do you want to know?"

"Your name, for starters."

"Vendelli. Frank Vendelli."

"See? We're off to a good start. Who hired you, Vendelli?"

"I don't know."

Hawker pointed the automatic at him.

"I *don't* know, goddamn it! Not really. I got a rep with some of the organizations that have holdings in Vegas, see? Sometimes these organizations have a problem with an organization member. Or they need some employee convinced that stealing isn't such a wise thing to do. Or maybe some out-of-town reporter comes snooping around, digging where he shouldn't ought to dig. Then they get in touch with me. There's no person-to-person contact. Just a phone call. They tell me who to hit, where I can find them and how heavy I should come down. I give them a location to drop the money. Hell, it could be any one of two dozen syndicates—or maybe an outside company, for all I know. Like I said, there's no personal contact. I work alone on my rep. I hire my own muscle—like Louie there."

"You said these people were animals. How do you know that if you don't know what organization you're working for?"

"Because of the way the guy on the phone told me to hit you."

"He told you my name? He told you where you could find me?"

"Yeah. He called a couple of hours ago. Said you'd be driving out this way."

"Did you recognize the voice? Had you ever heard it before?"

"No. Never. I'd remember, 'cause he had some kind of accent."

"What kind of accent?"

33

"How in the hell should I know? He wasn't from the Bronx. That's all I can tell you."

"Did he say what kind of car I'd be driving?"

"No. Just described you. Reddish brown–haired man traveling alone. Said I was to hit you just as hard as I could. Make it last. He said he wanted them to find you in pieces. Small pieces. Said he wanted to make an example of you."

"Did the same voice on the phone hire you to kill Jason Stratton?"

"Who?"

"A guy who lived in a cabin back down the mountain."

"I don't know nothing about that. But I'm not the only contract man in Vegas. There's not that much business anymore, but there's still a couple of others who like to keep their hands in."

"Fraternal organization of hired murderers, huh? Do you guys hold meetings and do charity work, too? Maybe show color slides at your get-togethers?"

"Hey, I wasn't going to slice you up," Vendelli said quickly. "Hell, that kind of shit left Vegas when Bugsy Siegel's partners from the Flamingo Hotel blew his brains out back in 1946. That crazy Jew liked to have his enemies cut up. Liked to send their families pieces of the body in the mail. Sure, I was going to hit you hard, buddy. My rep is built on successful contracts. But I was going to make it fast and clean. Hell, you wouldn't have felt a thing—if we'd caught you."

"I'm touched," said Hawker. "You're a real human being."

"I got my principles. I'm no geek. With me, it's a business." The man squirmed uncomfortably beneath the twisted steering wheel. "How about it, huh? I talked. Now get me the hell out of here."

Hawker nodded. "I'll get a crowbar from my car and see what I can do. I'd hate to see Las Vegas lose one of its most enterprising businessmen. But first, reach into the backseat and throw that rifle out the window."

Vendelli turned painfully and tossed the rifle away. "There. Now get me the hell out!"

Hawker went back to the Jaguar and opened the trunk. It took him a few minutes to find what he was looking for. The Jag had the complicated English jacking system, and the "crowbar" was little more than an L-shaped steel rod.

It would have to do.

Hawker shut the trunk and turned.

Facing him was Frank Vendelli.

The story about being trapped beneath the steering wheel had been a tale contrived to extend his life, to give him time. And James Hawker had fallen for it.

Hawker swore softly. While he was getting the jack, he had holstered the Walther.

Now he stood unarmed before the man who had been hired to kill him.

Vendelli leaned heavily against the wreckage of the Datsun. At least one of his legs was broken. Hawker wondered how he had gotten out of the wreck so quietly. Crawled through the window, he guessed.

In Vendelli's right hand was a .45-caliber ACP. Slowly he raised it toward Hawker.

As he did, Vendelli gave him a look of contempt. "You got

no reason to sneer at me, buddy. Sure, I'm a hired killer. But what are you? A cop, that's my guess. Maybe a federal cop. No, my connection on the phone didn't say anything about it. But you got that look about you. You handle yourself too well; you touch all the bases. A fed cop with a lot of experience, that's my guess. I've seen your kind before. CIA, maybe. One of those internal dudes who run deep cover. That's so you can kill and not have the heat come back on the feds if you get caught." He slung away more blood and sneered. "We both kill for dough, buddy. The only difference is, the organization you work for has more weight to toss around. But this time, my team wins."

Hawker had gauged the distance between them. Fifty feet, maybe. Less than the distance between home plate and the pitcher's mound. Even so, he needed to get closer if he was to have a chance. He knew he had to get Vendelli to keep talking if he was to succeed. But Vendelli was a pro. Killing people was his business.

It wouldn't be easy.

Hawker could only hope that the shock of the accident and the loss of blood had made him sloppy.

"You're wrong about my being a cop, Vendelli," Hawker said, walking forward as he spoke. "The people who own the Five-Cs complex brought me in. Someone is trying to force them out, and they want to find out why. That's why I'm here."

Vendelli shrugged. "Private investigator, cop—all the same thing. It makes no difference to me, buddy. I get paid the same no matter what you do."

"How much are they paying you, Vendelli? Whatever it is,

the guys at the Five-Cs will pay you more. They want to nail the bastards who are strongarming them."

The killer shook his head. "No deal. I've got a reputation, remember. That means I don't change horses. If I accept a job, I complete the job." He wiped more blood from his face and drew back the hammer of the .45 automatic. "So this is the end of the line for you, buddy. You're good, but you gave me an opening. And one opening is all Frank Vendelli needs." He leveled the gun. "Have a nice trip—to hell. . . ."

In one smooth motion, Hawker threw the jack handle as hard as he could while diving forward.

There was the explosion of a gunshot as Hawker somersaulted and came to his feet, the Walther PPK drawn.

He did not need it.

Hawker had played two seasons of pro ball; played for the Detroit organization in Lakeland, Florida, before being released because of a common baseball malady: an inability to hit the curve ball.

But he had always had an arm like a cannon.

The jack handle had hit Vendelli nose-high. The sharp end of the steel rod had gouged a furrow along his nose as if seeking a softer point of entry.

It had found it.

The jack handle had buried itself in the socket of the man's right eye, skewering through to the brain.

Frank Vendelli lay unmoving on the ground, dead.

Without pulling the jack handle free, Hawker wiped his prints clean. Then he laboriously dragged both corpses to the car and positioned them in the wrecked 280Z.

He hated to lose the Walther, but he had no choice. Besides, he had a duplicate back in the armament crates in his suite in Vegas.

He wiped his prints off the automatic, then placed it in Vendelli's right hand. He took both the .45 ACP and the .38.

As an afterthought, Hawker went through the billfolds of both men. Between them, they had two thousand dollars in cash.

Hawker left them with enough money so it would not look as if they had been robbed, then climbed back into the Jag.

It took him nearly a half-hour to find the old man who had been herding the sheep.

The old man was in the high pasture above the mountain road, patting down a mound of earth with a shovel.

There were tears in his eyes.

When Hawker pushed the wad of bills into his hand, he dropped the money on the ground and turned away.

"I lived with that old dog twelve years," the old man said in a choked voice, "and your money don't mean a goddamn thing to me. Just go on back to Vegas with the other hot-rod hotshots. You bastards have done nothing but screw up this state since you started coming here."

With no argument to offer in his favor, Hawker walked wordlessly to the Jaguar and drove back down the mountain to Jason Stratton's cabin.

FIVE

Jason Stratton's cabin looked more like a hermitage than a home.

It was built beneath trees on a bluff that overlooked a lonely gorge.

Stratton had used logs from the property, hand-chinked and mortared with homemade adobe. The roof was low, shingled with natural shakes. There were two cane-bottom chairs on the porch, and a hand pump for water outside.

The Nevada wind and sun had weathered the cabin nicely. It looked silver beneath the cool green of the trees.

Far beyond the rocky gorge was the smog stain of Las Vegas.

The porch creaked beneath Hawker's weight, and the plank door swung open at his touch.

What he saw inside surprised him.

A girl who couldn't have been more than twenty-four or twenty-five sat cross-legged on the bed. She had very long white-blond hair. She was gazing through the window at the gorge outside.

She also happened to be completely naked.

The girl turned when Hawker came in. But she didn't seem to be surprised, or uncomfortable at being naked. There was no hasty retreat, no anxious covering of her privates.

Instead, she smiled at him. "Hello," she said. "Are you looking for Jason?"

She had a bright, girlish face and very fair skin. The mouth was a little small for the plumpness of her lips. It gave her a poutish look. Her breasts were small, shaped like champagne glasses, and her nipples were pale pink. Hawker noted that the hair beneath her arms was only slightly darker than the hair on her head and the spun-glass triangle between her thighs.

"Am I looking for Jason?" Hawker repeated, realizing it had been long seconds since she had asked the question. "In a way. But I had no idea you were in here. I'm sorry. I should have knocked."

The girl continued to smile as she looked carefully at Hawker. "You're not a friend of Jason's, are you?"

"No. I've never met him. But how did you know?"

She shrugged and turned once again to the window. "I've never seen you around before. And you don't seem the type."

"Oh? And what type is that?"

The girl laughed. "You know. Your suit and tie. And driving up here in a fancy sports car."

"You saw me drive up?"

"No, but I heard the mufflers and I knew it was either a big motorcycle or a sports car. And you're not dusty enough to have been on a bike."

"Elementary, huh, Watson?"

The girl flopped around on the bed, grinning at him. "Hey, are you a Sherlock Holmes fan? I got on a real Holmes kick about a year ago. Read all fifty-six short stories and all three novellas."

"Four novellas," Hawker corrected.

"You *are* a Sherlockian." She slid off the bed and held out her hand. "I'm Wendy Nierson."

Hawker introduced himself and took her hand, doing his best to look her in the eye.

For the first time, she seemed to remember that she had no clothes on. "Say, does it bother you, my being naked? I'm so used to it, I forget that it can make other people uptight."

"Used to it? Are you a dancer in Vegas or something?"

For her age, she had an incongruously husky laugh. "Me? In Vegas? That's a good one. No, I live in a camp across the ridge. There are about thirty of us. Like a commune. We're nudists."

"A nudist camp."

"Yeah, but it's a lot more than that. We're really like a family. A real commune. We've got a cook house, a gigantic garden, a workshop, a school for the kids. That's how I got to know Jason. He came and taught the earth sciences. Biology, geology, botany. Even taught a basic business class once—the adults loved that. I've always been heavy into meditation, and he told me what a great place this cabin was to sit in. Meditate, I mean. And he was right. Really good vibes up here. Clears the mind and opens it right up to all the wavelengths most people forget they can listen to." She released his hand and looked at him with sly blue eyes. "So that leaves you. Why are you up here?"

"Like I said: looking for Jason."

Nonchalantly she opened a wooden chest and pawed through

a mound of clothes until she found a shirt. She put the shirt on, but didn't bother to button it. "Looking for Jason, huh?"

"Yes."

She cocked her head slightly. "Why are you lying to me? It's not necessary."

"But I'm not lying, Wendy."

"No? But you know Jason is dead."

"Do I?"

"Your mind tells me you do."

"So now you're a mind reader, too."

"With some people, I am." She nodded as if the knowledge still impressed even her. "Some people block me out entirely. But not you. I picked up the vibes from you the moment you walked in."

Hawker wondered why he was beginning to feel so uncomfortable. To cover his uneasiness, he pulled out a wooden chair and sat down. "And what do my vibes tell you, Wendy?"

She could have taken his tone as the lightest sarcasm, but she didn't. The blond girl thought hard for a moment. "I sense a lot of goodness in you. I felt immediate trust for you—if I hadn't, I'd have gotten the hell out the moment you came in. I always follow my instincts, James."

"Well, I'm flattered, Wendy—"

She held up her hands, cutting him off. "Don't talk. You asked me what kind of vibes I picked up, and I want to tell you as clearly as I can." She rolled her head back, loosening her neck muscles. "That's the first thing I felt: that goodness in you. But then I began to get a lot of dark stuff. Evil. It kind of scared me at first. That's when I asked if you were a friend of Jason's. If you had said yes, I would have left. I'd have known you were lying. But then I began to realize that none of that dark stuff, that evil, was directed at me." She looked at Hawker innocently. "It's kind of confusing, huh?"

"Yeah," James Hawker said. "It is."

"You've killed people, haven't you? A lot of people."

Confronted with her total openness, Hawker couldn't lie. "Yes, Wendy, I have."

"Like in a war or something?"

"Yes. A war. In a way."

"And they were bad people? Evil people?"

"I hope so, Wendy. Sometimes I worry I've made mistakes, but I don't think I have."

She nodded as if accepting that. "And now you've come to find the men who murdered Jason. And when you find them, you plan to kill them?"

"Not if I can help it. I don't really know."

She stood abruptly and bent over Hawker. She kissed him very tenderly on the lips. Then she opened the door to leave. "I hope you don't find them, James Hawker. I hope you don't find them, because I picked up something else in the vibes. Something bad. Something very bad."

Hawker was still thinking about the extraordinary softness of her lips. "And what's that, Wendy?"

"It's death, James. Your death. I sense that you are to die soon. Maybe not this week; maybe not even this year. But soon. Too soon."

As she stepped onto the porch and trotted into the yard, she called over her shoulder, "I live just over that ridge, James. I hope you'll come and see me. Any time, day or night, it doesn't matter. You'll be welcome. . . ."

Hawker sat unmoving for several minutes. He had met the hippie types before: the whole cast of pot smokers, meditators, bead weavers, free livers, pseudo-intellectuals and the general run of drug-damaged do-nothings all of those things implied.

But still, Wendy Nierson didn't seem to fit neatly into those categories. Her openness, her honesty, in fact, seemed to put her above the narrow cubbyholing of human types.

Hawker thought about her for a while longer, then stood. He had work to do. He had come to search Jason Stratton's cabin, not waste time wondering about one woman's surprising display of extrasensory perception.

So he did just that: searched the cabin.

There was surprisingly little dust about for a place supposedly vacant for several weeks. But that could have been because Wendy had been using it, keeping it clean.

Stratton seemed to have few material belongings. The books on the shelves over the bed were mostly nonfiction. Academic works on biology, geology, the arts.

He had made a table out of planking and cement blocks. On the table were a microscope, a few jars of chemicals, then a long row of jars. In the jars, soaking in formaldehyde, were various species of spiders, insects and snakes.

Hawker looked closely at the jars of chemicals. Because they were not labeled, he found some envelopes and took samples of each.

Also on the table was a display case of rocks. Many were

quite beautiful: raw crystals of red, blue, green and clear white. Another looked like salt crystals immersed in shiny black tar. Some were labeled with their scientific names. Others weren't. Outside the display case were mounds of other rocks, beside which were a geologist's hammer and a stone polishing machine.

He put samples of the rocks in separate envelopes.

Hawker knew that almost everyone had a secret hiding place: a place to stash money, private papers, diaries.

He spent half an hour looking for Stratton's before he found it: inside the wall behind a broken board.

There was $732 in cash, a life insurance policy and a notebook.

Hawker put it all in a manila envelope, then climbed back into the Jaguar and took his time driving back to Las Vegas, enjoying the scenery he had missed on the trip out.

SIX

Half an hour late, Barbara Blaine parted the crowd in the elegant Mirage dining room as with a wave of her hand.

She singled out Hawker sitting in a far corner and allowed the maître d' to escort her to the table.

Hawker had expected a gaudier woman. A woman who, because of her unusual social position, cultivated a go-to-hell look through loud clothes, heavy makeup, bright colors and an avante garde hairstyle.

He was pleasantly surprised.

Everything about Barbara Blaine was subtle, understated. She was one of the long, lithe ones. A hint of Mediterranean in the glossy black hair, the hollow cheeks and the penetrating brown eyes. A suggestion of the athlete in the fluidity of her walk. The implication of the successful business-person in the assertive movements, the no-nonsense gaze above the winning smile.

Her evening gown was held by a single shoulder strap, the gown a silver satin creation that flowed down over the svelte swell of breasts, the flexing convexity of buttocks, the sleek brown legs. She carried the small pearl handbag as naturally as, Hawker was sure, she would carry an expensive briefcase.

He found himself standing at her approach. Her handshake was dry, firm and brief. A chairman-of-the-board handshake.

"I'm late," she said. It was not an apology. It was a statement.

"I thought no one looked at clocks in Las Vegas," Hawker said as they took their seats.

"Oh, there are still a few of us who haven't fallen under the spell of complete and unremitting debauchery." She gave him a careful look as she opened the velvet menu proffered by the maître d'.

"I'm nursing a beer, Barbara. Drink?"

"I shouldn't, but I will. It's been one of those damn crazy days." She gave her order to the waiter rather than Hawker. "Billy, I want the biggest, driest, coldest martini that rummy bartender of yours can build. Let me work on it for about twenty minutes, then bring me an artichoke salad—double portion—and a pot of coffee. Sweet 'n Low but no cream."

"Right away, Miss Blaine."

Her order was given so succinctly that the waiter got halfway to the kitchen before remembering he had failed to get Hawker's dinner order.

Hawker ordered the onion soup, prime rib au jus, baron cut, a dish of cold asparagus with mayonnaise and a double order of garlic toast.

When he had finished, he folded the menu and turned his attention to the woman across the table from him.

"It was nice of you to agree to this meeting," he said.

"Nothing nice about it," she countered. "Kevin Smith says you might be able to help us. I have no intention of selling the Doll House, and I don't care to spend the next year living in fear for the lives of my friends. If you can help us, I will cooperate in any way I can."

"You play the part of the steely businesswoman very nicely."

"Maybe I'm not playing a part. Maybe I'm just that: steely." The waiter brought her martini. She tasted it experimentally and nodded that it was satisfactory. She spun the swizzle stick in her fingers as she continued. "And I am a businesswoman, Mr. Hawker. Even in my business, people who see me rarely mistake me for anything else. But I must admit that you look nothing like I pictured you."

"Oh?"

"Not at all. I guess I expected the Sam Spade type. Cheap suit frayed at the elbows. Rough complexion. Cigarette sticking out of the corner of your mouth. A bulge under your lapel where your gun is holstered. Glassy scars on your jaws and knuckles." She peered at him closely over the candle in the center of the table. "But I guess you do have a few scars, don't you?"

"A few. I hope they make up for the other shortcomings."

She laughed. "Oh, I'm not disappointed in you. Not yet. Kevin Smith speaks highly of your abilities." Her gaze narrowed. "In fact, he said you were something of a legend among the major police departments in this country. He said he had never even met you before yesterday, yet he was sure you were the ideal man for the job when he realized that neither he nor the official police could handle it. I wonder why, Mr. Hawker. Why would one man be able to succeed where a whole force of trained policemen might fail?"

Hawker shrugged. "To begin with, I'm not Mr. Hawker. That was my father. I'm 'James' or 'Hawk' or just about anything else you care to call me. And maybe it's because I don't take coffee breaks. And I don't have a union that charges time and a half. And, of course, there are no guarantees I won't fail. Working undercover offers certain advantages, but it also makes me more vulnerable."

"Is that right? For some reason, you don't strike me as the vulnerable type."

"I become especially vulnerable when the people I'm after have a spy in my own camp."

She put down her drink quickly, her face incredulous. "What? You can't mean that."

Hawker shrugged. "Today on the telephone, I told you I planned to check out Jason Stratton's cabin this afternoon. I left a note for Captain Smith telling him the same thing. Through one of those two sources, the organization trying to force you out of your businesses was informed."

"I didn't tell a damn soul!"

"I'm not saying you did. It was stupid of me to leave the information in a note. Anyone could have opened it, read it, then put it in a fresh envelope. It's a mistake I will never make again."

"Or the telephone lines could have been tapped," Barbara Blaine said thoughtfully.

Hawker nodded. "Or they could have bugged my room. I didn't have time to give it a thorough going over when I returned late this afternoon, but I will tonight."

"But they knew where you were going? And they followed you?"

Hawker poured the rest of his Tuborg into the pilsner glass.

He didn't want to go into too much detail. For one thing, he had no real proof that he could trust this woman. On the way out to Vegas, he had formed several possible scenarios to explain the extortion attempt on the Five-Cs complex. One of the scenarios was that Jason Stratton hadn't been murdered—he had disappeared voluntarily to work undercover against the Five-Cs with his accomplice, Barbara Blaine.

The scenario didn't seem to fit now. Barbara Blaine seemed too earnest; the things he had found in Stratton's cabin suggested that he had, indeed, been kidnapped or murdered.

Even so, Hawker omitted some key information from his story. He had learned very quickly that in Las Vegas, the opposition only needs one small opening to kill you.

She listened transfixed to the story of the car chase. "But what happened after they wrecked their car?" she demanded. "Did they talk? Did they say anything?"

Hawker looked at her levelly. "They were both killed."

Her hand trembled slightly as she touched the martini glass to her lips. "They were killed? In the car wreck, you mean?"

"In the paper tomorrow you will read that the two men somehow got into a fight with each other while driving through Kyle Canyon. The police will be confused, so they will say that it is still under investigation. But they will decide the two men killed each other. The car, of course, then went out of control and wrecked."

"*You* killed them," she whispered.

Hawker looked away noncommittally.

"But did they tell you anything first? Did you find out who hired them—"

"No. They didn't grant me an interview. They were too busy trying to convert me into a corpse so they could dump me and my car into the canyon."

"My God," she said. "Then I . . . I was right. Jason is . . . they really did kill him?"

"I think so. I found evidence in his cabin that he did not leave voluntarily."

"Oh, no," she whispered. "That's awful. It didn't seem so hard to accept when I was the only one insisting he had been murdered. I guess it was because deep in my heart, I secretly believed I was wrong. But to hear you say it . . ."

The woman whimpered, and her chest heaved as she fought for control. Hawker reached over and patted her hand. "Maybe we should eat later. Let's go up to my suite. I have a few things I need to show you, and it'll give you time to calm down."

"Yes," she said quickly. "That might be best."

Hawker found their waiter and gave him a twenty to delay their dinner orders, then took Barbara Blaine's hand and led her through the casino to the elevator.

This was a different woman from the one who had entered the dining room with such quiet flair. Now she was soft and vulnerable and very, very damn close to breaking.

The change was so drastic and so touching that Hawker found himself feeling sorry for her.

Like the hard-nosed whorehouse matrons of fiction, this one really did seem to have a tender heart made for breaking.

SEVEN

Back in his suite, Hawker poured gin into a beaker and added the obligatory scent of vermouth. He filled the beaker with ice, shook it and served the martini in a chilled glass with a triple portion of olives.

Barbara Blaine took the drink gratefully.

"Better?"

She nodded. "I don't understand why it hit me so hard all of a sudden." She looked out the broad veranda window and spoke out loud, as if listening to her own words. "Jason is dead. Jason Stratton is dead." She shivered and took down half the drink in a gulp. "And it's such a damnable waste."

Hawker took the manila envelope from the desk. He opened it and handed it to her. "I found this stuff hidden in his cabin. If he had left voluntarily, he would have taken it."

She looked at the wad of bills for a moment and smiled wryly at some private memory. She put the money on the bed with the insurance policy. Then she turned her attention to the journal: a small book bound in black leather.

She leafed through the pages, then looked at Hawker. "I've seen him carry this. He used to joke about it. Of course, with Jason, it was hard to tell when he was joking and when he wasn't. He used to say this would be his doctoral dissertation, but that no one would understand it. Now I see why."

Hawker didn't have to ask what she was talking about. He had already looked at the journal. There were about three hundred pages covered in a minute, carefully written code. There were drawings of plants and insects, and a few entries in recognizable English, but most of it was in what seemed to be a random combination of numbers and letters.

"I was hoping he had explained the code to you. You seem to think these people killed Jason as a way to pressure you. I'm not so sure."

"But why in the hell else would they do it?" she snapped. "He was such a kind . . . good . . . person. Jason wouldn't hurt anybody. It wasn't in him."

Hawker shrugged. "Maybe he saw something he shouldn't have. Maybe he knew something they didn't want him to know. I was hoping you or this journal could tell me a little more about him."

"All I know about the code he used is something he told me about his boyhood. He came from a big family with a drunken, nosy mother. He said he developed the code when he was in his teens, so she couldn't read what he had written. He said he'd been using it so long that it was second nature to write that way."

"He never hinted at the key to the code?"

Barbara Blaine thought for a moment, then gave a negative shake of her head. She began to riffle through her handbag. "Do you have any cigarettes?"

"No."

She put down the bag and returned to her drink. "I don't either. I quit two years ago—when I met Jason. But sometimes I still carry them for friends—and to prove I don't need them. He had this way about him, a way of making you not only believe in him but in yourself, too. I mentioned once that I wanted to quit smoking, and then very calmly and very kindly he told me all this scientific stuff about cigarettes. He explained that no one really enjoyed sucking poison into their lungs; that claiming to enjoy it was really just a rationalization for the physical feelings of addiction. He asked me to picture how ridiculous I looked sucking a white stick of burning leaves. He said it was the tobacco industry—a multibillion-dollar industry—that had replaced the honestly absurd image of smoking with a carefully planned image of sophistication and sexuality. He said I was allowing them to use me as a dupe. A slave, really, who earned them several hundred dollars a year in profit—not to mention the grave harm I was doing to my own body. Jason didn't lecture people. He reasoned with them. He got me so mad at my own silliness and at the tobacco industry that I quit that afternoon."

Hawker waited patiently, knowing the woman had to work into it in her own way.

She swirled the gin in the glass, staring deeply into the clarity of it. "I met him just over two years ago. I had just built the Doll House, had just built on property I'd bought from the Five-Cs syndicate. Outwardly I was feeling very proud of myself. Very tough and in control. The house was tastefully done, and I had built it all myself. No partners. And I knew that I would soon be rich, have all the money I had ever dreamed of.

"But inwardly I felt . . . I felt just as cheap and dirty as a person can feel." She looked up at Hawker suddenly. "Do you want to know how I became the matron of a whorehouse? Take the most obvious guess, and you'll be right. I worked on my own, free-lance, for three years. A thousand dollars a night—and I did my best to make damn sure I was worth it. I read all the literature, learned all the tricks and then improved on them. If a man paid me once, I did anything I had to do to make sure he would be back. I got the occasional sicko. I was beaten badly twice. But I went right back to work when I got out of the hospital. For an attractive woman from a poor background, there are only two ways to get rich, Hawk. One way is to marry a rich man." She laughed sardonically. "That's the most common form of prostitution, isn't it? But I didn't want a bad husband and a bad marriage. I had watched a bad marriage turn my mother into an old and broken woman. But I did want to be rich. Money was power, and I wanted power. So I chose the other form of prostitution.

"I told myself I was just being a tough businesswoman. I had a product that men were willing to pay dearly for. So I exploited it. In those three years, I grossed $463,500. I didn't make the common mistake of not declaring my earnings to the IRS. I reported every cent, paid the taxes, saved every remaining dollar. I told myself I could quit when I had a quarter of a million. After three years as a whore, after paying taxes and living expenses and making some wise investments, I had saved $305,000. It was all the money I needed to start my own business. I had seen the ruin of too many fellow prostitutes, and, like I said, I'd spent some time in the hospital myself. So I decided to start my own house. A classy place that was safe and carefully monitored. A whorehouse run like a first-rate business firm. The girls in my house have a damn good retirement plan. I strongly encourage them to take a sizable portion of their earnings and pool it in money market accounts or CDs or bonds. If they want to continue their education, the house pays seventy-five percent of the tab. Drugs kill more prostitutes than sickos, so the first thing I did was set up a drug rehab program. Every one of my girls is clean. So you see, Hawk, I was a whore before I became a rich businesswoman." Her tight smile was like a challenge. "Are you shocked?"

Hawker shook his head. "Like you said, there are many forms of prostitution. I imagine most junior executives in major firms compromise themselves more often than an average prostitute. Why should I be shocked?"

The woman looked at him carefully. "For just a moment there, I thought I was hearing Jason again."

"Which is exactly what I need you to talk about."

Barbara Blaine finished her drink, laughing. "God, I got carried away, didn't I?" She found the martini pitcher and poured herself another drink. "But it all has to do with the way I met Jason and why I was attracted to him."

"He wasn't a . . . he didn't come to your house—"

"Jason visit a whorehouse? You would have had to know him to know just how funny that question is. Jason is . . . was a pure spirit. An intellectual who loved the clarity of science. The absent-minded-professor type. He was very bright and very naive, and I grew to love him dearly. The way I met him, the Doll House was just nearing completion. It's about a mile from here and, like the casinos, there's nothing else around it. Just the neatly landscaped lawn out front, and sagebrush behind. I was in the house one afternoon, and I saw this stranger lurking around out back. On my property! With all the pomp and severity of a new landowner, I charged right out and asked him just what in the hell he was doing on my property. He had this shoddy canvas knapsack he always carried, and he had one of those funny-shaped hammers that rock collectors carry. I bawled him out good, lecturing him about trespassing and snooping and God knows what else. Like all whores, I guess, I had come to hate men, and I didn't want to miss the opportunity to put this man in his place. But he just stood there, smiling kind of shyly, and when I was done, he held out this pasty-colored rock. He asked me to look at it. I came very close to slapping it out of his hand and calling the police. But instead I took it and looked. I spent the next two years secretly thanking myself for looking at that rock.

"On the outside, it was just a plain old rock. But inside was the perfect outline of an animal. Some kind of fish. Very delicate and very pretty. Jason began talking about that fossil. He told me that thousands of years ago, the land the Five-Cs complex was built on had been a riverbed. He said it was a big raging river that flowed to the sea. By that time, I had him marked as some kind of kook. Tall and blond, with glasses. Kind of gangly and boyish-looking, but harmless. I no longer had any interest in men in a physical sense. Even so, he was kind of attractive in a funny way. He made me feel like he needed protecting or something. So I listened to him talk about the fossil, and before I knew it, what he was saying was actually *interesting*. I had gone right from high school to being a Las Vegas showgirl, and then to being a Vegas whore, so I was academically ignorant. He made all that stale stuff come alive. I could actually *see* this river flowing where my business now was. He talked about the geological formation of the mountains, and about the dinosaurs and jungles that once covered Nevada. The things he talked about made me realize for the first time how . . . insignificant my own problems and accomplishments were. It did something to me. I can't explain it. I guess it was because it made all the guilt I felt at being a whore seem ridiculously unimportant and small. Then all of a sudden I started to cry. I don't know why. I couldn't stop crying. Jason bundled me into his car and drove me up into the mountains to his cabin. He made tea for me and then listened to me talk. I must have talked nonstop for three hours. I told him everything."

Barbara Blaine looked up at Hawker uncomfortably. "I know it must sound odd, my going off and talking to a complete stranger. But I had no male friends. A whore can't afford male friends, you see. And Jason had this knack for making strangers feel completely and totally at ease. He listened like what you said was the most important thing in the world. Jason had a very real magic about him. Everyone who ever met him felt it. Whenever someone was in trouble or had a problem, they came to Jason to sort it out."

"And you became lovers?"

She shook her head quickly. "Not at first. I had been a whore, remember? I had already had intercourse with three hundred and seventeen different men by actual count. All kinds of men—fat, thin, white, black, big, little and in between. And I despised every one of them. To me, sex was work, a bit of theater to be performed nude. I took no pleasure in it. Maybe that's why I felt so comfortable with Jason. He never once made a pass at me. Never once said anything suggestive. When I saw him, it was usually to go on collecting trips. He called me his pack mule, because I carried whatever he happened to be collecting at the time. We talked a lot. We talked about everything. He opened my eyes to a lot of things: science, history, religion. I stayed up there in his cabin with him sometimes. I slept in the bed, and he slept outside on the porch because he said he loved sleeping outside. It was all very open and innocent, and very damn good for me. I hate to think what I would have turned into if it hadn't been for Jason Stratton."

The woman shivered slightly, thinking about it. Then she began to talk once again, with the same faraway look in her eyes, remembering. "When we finally did become lovers, I had to initiate it. I was staying at the cabin. It was very late, and it began to rain. Really pour. Jason was sleeping outside, as usual. I got up to check on him. He was soaking wet. And shivering. It gets very damn cold up there. I helped him get out of his wet clothes, and I began to rub him dry with a blanket. I was wearing one of his T-shirts for a nightgown. While I dried him, I began to feel something. It was that funny feeling, low in the abdomen. It had been so long since I had felt it that it took me a moment to realize I was becoming sexually aroused. Jason, very obviously, was feeling the same way. We became lovers that night, Hawk, and I can honestly say that it was the first time in my life that I enjoyed it. It was wonderful because I *loved* him, you see. I really did. I couldn't get enough of Jason Stratton, and he felt the same way about me. We spent the next two days alone on that mountain, and I consider it one of the most wonderful times in my life. I knew then that I would be with that man always and forever, no matter what happened."

Hawker watched with admiration as Barbara Blaine fought the tears and won. She shifted her weight and continued. "He wanted to get married because he wanted kids. I did too, but not as the proprietor of a whorehouse. We decided that I would work for two years, sell the place, and then we would be financially set for the rest of our lives. Money meant nothing to him, but it was still important to me. And you have no idea how sorry I am now that we didn't just go ahead and become husband and wife."

"Did Jason know there were people trying to force you into selling the Doll House?"

She shook her head. "No. I kept my business dealings completely out of our relationship. He still came to the Doll House because of all the fossils left by the old river. The girls liked him and highly approved of our relationship. But we never discussed the business. He knew how uncomfortable it made me feel."

"Did the mob give you any indication they would take measures so drastic?"

She thought for a moment. "I guess they did. But I guess I just didn't believe their threats. It all started when two men came to the Doll House and asked to see me. They were dressed like they wanted to look important and respectable, but it made them look all the sleazier. They said they represented people who wanted to buy the Doll House. Because I wanted to marry Jason, I listened to the proposal. But their numbers were all wrong. They didn't want to buy the place, they wanted to steal it. I told them I wasn't interested. But they just sat there sort of smirking at me. They said I didn't understand. They said they weren't asking me if I wanted to sell. They were telling me I *had* to sell. I told them to get the hell out or I would call the police. They left, but those smirks never left their faces. After thinking about it, I decided to call the police anyway. I gave the police their names. The police checked into it."

Hawker guessed what had happened. "The police couldn't do anything because the men had given you fake names and, besides, there were no witnesses to the threats."

"You've got it."

"When was that exactly?"

"Ah . . . about two months ago. Mid-June."

"The same time they tried to buy the Five-Cs complex."

"Yeah. And they pulled the same deal. Made Captain Smith and his associates a low offer. A very low offer. Two days after they refused, the threats started."

"What kind of threats?"

"Telephone threats. When they called here, they didn't even ask for me. They'd say stuff like, 'If your boss doesn't sell, a lot of you girls are going to see the inside of a hospital.' The worst thing was the way they disguised their voices. They used weird accents. It scared the hell out of my girls. And it scared me, too."

"But they never actually did anything?"

"We've had some broken windows. And three weeks ago, someone tried to torch the place. But I've got a damn good security system, and the sensors picked up the smoke in plenty of time. And you know about how Charlie Kullenburg was beaten up. Three men in stocking masks. They robbed him, but Captain Smith thinks it was so the police would treat it like a regular holdup. That was three weeks ago—just before Jason disappeared. After that, my girls have been afraid to leave the house. I don't blame them. And we've been keeping an especially close eye on our clients."

Hawker was surprised. "You can do that?"

Barbara Blaine nodded and stood. "So far, James, all you've seen is my soft side. Maybe it's because you're easy to talk to. But I've got another side, too."

"So I've heard."

"Walk me back to the Doll House and I'll show you. We can have dinner there, and I can tell you more about Jason." She gave him a look of quick appraisal. "Then, if you like, I can fix you up with one of the girls."

"Dinner will be enough."

Barbara Blaine smiled. "Don't decide too quickly. You haven't seen my girls yet."

EIGHT

The Doll House was a three-story white clapboard reproduction of an eighteenth-century mansion.

It had the look of a small estate that had been modernized and turned into a business. Green shutters on the windows, a porch with pillars, lighted fountain in the front yard surrounded by formal plantings. The small parking lot and the walk to the front door were shielded by a high copse.

And Barbara Blaine's girls truly were spectacular.

It was a Wednesday night, a slow night, according to Barbara. In Vegas, the junket masters usually arranged for gamblers to arrive on a Thursday or Friday. They flew them out on a Monday or Tuesday.

In Vegas, Wednesday was the equivalent of Sunday in most other towns.

Barbara took him in through the front door. The foyer was manned by a balding bouncer with football-size biceps. Barbara patted him on the shoulder, and the bouncer lowered his eyes and smiled like a grateful pup.

The interior was a masterpiece of decoration, lighting and efficiency. Chandeliers draped from high ceilings. Plush carpet and velvet divans. Tasteful nudes done in oils or sculpted marble. Two sitting rooms. The first was less formal. A full bar. An antique jukebox loaded only with classics from the Big Band era and a few light opera pieces. Tables for eating and drinking. A tile floor for dancing.

The other sitting room was kept in a softer light. This would be where the men would make their selections. Velvet chairs positioned near windows, like a photographer's still-life. Ornate floor lamps with golden bulbs. A *Gone With the Wind* stairway that led upstairs to the private rooms. An intercepting desk with a leather receipt book and a credit card roller.

American Express. Don't leave home without it.

But on this night, a slow night, Barbara Blaine's girls were enjoying themselves in the least formal of the two rooms. They carried drinks in tall glasses, and the jukebox vibrated with "Boogie Woogie Bugle Boy."

There were thirteen of them. Striking blondes, leggy brunettes, busty girls of glistening ebony.

They wore pants suits or short shorts and halters, and they laughed uproariously.

Hawker had seen plenty of whores in his time—and too often, they were facedown in some back alley, beaten to death. Or eternally asleep in their own bathtubs, wrists slit.

The whores he had seen were creatures of the night; the streetwalkers with tawdry tight dresses, cheap flaxen wigs, gaudy makeup and bright lipstick.

But the girls of the Doll House looked like no prostitutes he had ever seen before. They looked like they had been shipped to Vegas from some Midwestern beauty show. They were ripe and lovely, and their hair and skin glistened with health.

Barbara Blaine called for attention and introduced Hawker. She introduced him as an "old friend," which, Hawker noted, seemed to tell the girls he was not a potential customer. They filed past one by one to shake his hand. Their smiles were warm, the hand contact tempting. More than one of the girls gave him a burning look and a meaningful extra squeeze of the palm.

Barbara Blaine raised her eyebrows, asking Hawker for his reaction.

"I'm speechless," he said with a laugh.

"They *are* beautiful, aren't they?"

"It boggles the mind. I had no idea."

"But they're more than just beautiful, James. They're smart. These girls have the looks to be film stars or big-league dancers, but they don't have the talent. It's not their fault. They just didn't happen to be blessed with the abilities they need. But unlike too many tragic women, these girls have the brains to admit to themselves that they would never get past the casting couch in Vegas or Hollywood. So they've come here. And believe me, I only select the best. I check their records clear back to grade school. We don't want any neurotics or drug addicts here. I want clean, healthy girls who have the emotional stability to deal with the trauma of being a high-class whore. And it is traumatic, James. I can testify to that.

"We sign a two-year contract. They can leave anytime they wish before the two years are up. But, at the end of the two years, they *must* leave for their own well-being. Each girl makes a minimum of a hundred thousand a year, plus tips, so it comes out to more like a hundred and twenty thousand. Their room and board, hospitalization, social security and life insurance are covered by the house, so they don't have many outside expenses. I don't exactly force them to put the money into blue chip stock portfolios and CDs or bonds, but I make it clear that if they don't, they won't be working here long. So at the end of their two years, they leave with my very best wishes and about a quarter-million in cash. By that time, I've also made sure they have a few business courses under their belts."

Hawker gave a low whistle. "Now I can see why they're laughing."

The woman smiled, pleased that Hawker was impressed. "Follow me. I want to show off the rest of the place."

"There's more?"

"You've seen the icing. Now I want to show you the cake."

Hawker followed her through a side hall that went through a small but modern kitchen that was all tile and stainless steel. The chef was a tiny man in white with a huge gray handlebar mustache. Barbara gave him their dinner order and then led Hawker to the back of the house.

Here the decorations were so different that they might have entered a separate building.

These were her living quarters, she explained, a house within a house. It was a one-bedroom suite with a den, a massive sunken living room and a wall of glass that looked out onto a tropical garden and swimming pool.

Hawker hummed and nodded his approval dutifully. "Not exactly a hand-built cabin on a mountain, is it?"

"Between the two, I preferred the cabin."

"That brings us back to Jason, Barbara. In the weeks before he disappeared, did he say or do anything unusual, anything out of character that suggested he might have found out about your problems?"

She thought for a long moment. "No. No, I don't think so. Actually we didn't get a chance to talk much during that last week. He was very busy working on one of his projects."

"What kind of project?"

"Something to do with fossils and rocks, that's all I know." She thought for a moment before adding, "He did say one thing that was rather odd. It was the last time I saw him, as a matter of fact. It was late in the morning, and he stopped at the house for something to drink. He seemed to be in a very good mood. He said that he thought his doctoral dissertation was going to be even better than he had hoped. He said it might make it possible for us to get married a lot sooner than we had planned. When I tried to press him for details, he just laughed and said he would tell me later."

"Did he say anything about having an appointment with anyone?"

"No. The police asked me the same thing."

"How did Jason get around? What kind of car did he drive?"

"A real old khaki jeep. He needed it for his work."

"Has the jeep been found?"

The woman shook her head. "No. I guess that's why I still had hope."

"When I visited Jason's cabin, I met a girl who said she was a member of some kind of commune not far from Jason's property. Did you or the police talk to them about Jason's disappearance?"

"The police did, and I did, too. They call themselves the Spring Mountain Family. They live the pure life. No drugs, no meat, homegrown vegetables—and no clothes. Jason liked them very much, and they liked him."

"And how do you feel about them?"

She shrugged. "Truthfully, they made me uncomfortable. I'm suspicious of extremist groups. Even the benevolent ones."

"Is there any chance they could have been responsible?"

"No, I don't think so. They loved Jason—or said they did. And they seemed awfully eager to help."

The woman placed her hands on her slim hips, a world-weary look on her face. Hawker sensed that she was tired of questions.

"Hungry?"

"Sure. But you asked how we could monitor the girls, Hawk. Let me show you; then we'll eat."

Hawker nodded and followed the woman to a room protected by a steel fire door. It took three keys to unlock it.

The room was a small fortress. The fluorescent lighting was built into the ceiling, and there were three banks of computer boards on metal desks. On the inboard side of the room was a walk-in safe built into the wall. Above the computer was a bank of lights and toggle switches, and three small television sets.

Barbara Blaine flipped some switches, and the TV screens came on. They showed the interiors of three different rooms. Each of the rooms had one large water bed. All the rooms were empty.

She touched another bank of switches, and three more rooms came into view.

One of these rooms was in use.

On the television screen, a silver-haired man in amazingly good shape sat beneath a young woman with startling mammary development. She hunched over his hips, ingurgitating him with all the precision of a German clock.

The man was smiling.

Barbara Blaine cleared her throat uncomfortably and blanked the screens.

"You could get sponsors. Start your own cable network."

"That joke's original only because I allow no one else in here. I check the beds visually only when I have reason to. I respect the girls' privacy and they know that, so they don't mind if I use discretion. Besides, the cameras only monitor the work rooms, not their private rooms. In each of the work rooms is a button hidden behind the head of each bed. If they press the button once, an internal alarm system is set off, and we immediately go to their aid. If they press it three times, the computer simultaneously dials the police and the emergency squad, and a prerecorded voice gives our address and requests immediate assistance."

"A real red alert, huh?"

"Thank God we haven't had occasion to use it yet. But if we need it, it's there. The girls know it, and it makes them feel a lot safer. I remember one time, about three months ago—" The woman stopped suddenly in mid-sentence, a look of concern clouding her face. She was staring at the bank of lights and toggle switches.

One of the marble-size lights was flashing.

A red light.

"What's wrong, Barbara?"

She shook her head and hit one of the toggles. "Something triggered one of the sensors out back. It alerts the computer, and the computer sets off chimes in my suite." She held her finger to her lips as she adjusted a volume knob. "Listen!"

At first, Hawker could hear nothing but the hollow buzz of the outdoor microphone. But then his ears focused on a familiar sound: the whispered grind of footsteps on gravel. Slow footsteps. Careful footsteps.

The woman left the volume on and reached for the telephone. "I'm calling the police, Hawk. Those bastards need to be stopped, and stopped now."

Hawker placed his hand over hers so she couldn't take the phone from the cradle. "No. Not yet. I'm going out there."

She grabbed his sleeve as she stepped toward the door. "Please don't, Hawk! You don't know how many of them there are. And they might have guns, for Christ's sake!"

The rush of adrenaline caused him to sweep her hand away harder than he had planned. "Have I criticized your business, told you how to run it, Barbara?"

"No . . . no, you haven't, Hawk."

"Then don't tell me how to run mine."

Hawker moved quickly down the hall into the main suite. He peered through the glass wall, let his eyes adjust to the shadows of tropical garden, the onyx mirror of swimming pool.

No one there.

Hawker patted his jacket, damning himself for not taking the time to replace the lost Walther with another from his armament store shipped to him by Jacob Montgomery Hayes.

Another mistake.

When in the hell had he become so sloppy?

Maybe it was the to-hell-with-tomorrow attitude carefully cultivated by the people of Las Vegas.

Whatever the reason, he had to get over it, get over it damn quick.

Or he would end up all too dead.

Hawker peeled his trouser leg up over his calf.

He still had the Randall Model 18 Attack/Survival.

And the Randall had pulled him through more than one tight spot.

Hawker balanced the cool steel of the knife in his right hand as he made his way through the living room to the side exit. He cracked the door open, then stepped through.

It was a clear Nevada night. An August night with low humidity and stars that glistened through the black light-years like ice shards. The desert wind was warm on his face, and he could smell the musk of the tropical garden and the chlorine odor of the swimming pool.

Hawker closed the door behind him and followed the stone walk to the back of the house. The walk was edged by some kind of tall African grass, higher than his head.

The landscaper had chosen river rock over sod for the back-yard. Less maintenance. The footfall they had heard had been in gravel.

Hawker knew the interloper was out back someplace. Someplace in the shadows; someplace waiting, watching.

It didn't take him long to find out exactly where.

Hawker heard a door creak open, and he turned to see Barbara Blaine peeking out. He had been crouched in the shadows, but now he stood to wave her back inside.

When he did, something hit him from behind. A man, hiding in the tall grass. A big man with a big belly and wide shoulders. A man who grunted and wheezed and smelled faintly of alcohol.

The impact knocked Hawker tumbling and whipped his neck back painfully.

But it didn't knock the knife from his hand.

The man stood glowering over Hawker. He raised his right hand—an aiming pose. In the darkness, the handgun looked more like a chunk of coal. Absently Hawker noticed that the man carried something beneath his left arm. Something the size of a shoebox.

And Hawker also realized that he was going to be shot. Realized there was nothing he could do about it. Saw it all as from some higher platform of observation: saw the gun lift toward him; saw himself sprawled on the gravel; knew the man could not miss at that range, even with a handgun.

In that microsecond of realization, it flashed into James Hawker's mind that Wendy Nierson, the blond-haired free spirit on the mountain, had been right.

He was to die.

Die all too soon.

NINE

Determined not to die meekly on the ground, Hawker made a desperate lunge toward the figure that stood before him.

He kept low, waiting for the heavy, impersonal impact of lead that would announce his own death.

But instead of a gunshot, there was a scream.

A woman's scream.

Somehow Barbara Blaine had gotten to his attacker. Even though he had waved her inside, she had followed him out. She had sprinted toward the gunman, her fingernails clawing at his eyes.

The man clubbed her solidly behind the ear, then turned his attention once again to Hawker.

But the woman's charge had given Hawker the extra second he needed.

As the gun came vectoring around, Hawker ducked under it and used his head to butt the man solidly in the solar plexus.

It should have knocked him to the ground. Instead, he hit the side of the house, and the clapboard walls kept him on his feet. He snapped off two quick shots. In the dry Nevada night, the gun sounded like the *kerWHACK* of a bullwhip.

Hawker felt a burning sensation in his ear. He wondered if he had been shot.

Hawker used his left elbow to knock the man's gun hand up and away—but too late. The man used the butt of the revolver like a sap, clubbing Hawker solidly behind the head. All the world went slow and dreamy for a moment; a world of bright popping lights; the red, green and yellow starburst world caused by a sudden cranial pressure trying to escape through the delicate aqueous jelly of cornea.

Somehow, the blow jarred the knife from his hands. It fell with a heavy metallic thud into the gravel.

And then the test of strength began. Hawker had both hands locked around the gun, trying to force the weapon up and away. His attacker had his left hand over Hawker's hands, trying to force the revolver down to face level. The man grunted and wheezed and groaned, but the match began to lean in Hawker's favor. Hawker sensed the knee snapping toward his groin, and he turned his thigh into the blow just in time.

The kick threw the man's balance off, and Hawker twisted the gun out of his hands. It flew in a high arc into the bushes.

The adrenaline rush of desperation had left Hawker now, leaving only a cold, cold fury.

This stranger had pistol-whipped the pretty lady. This stranger had tried to shoot him; had tried to kill him dead, dead, dead.

Hawker drew back his right fist and drove all his weight behind it. The fist collided with the man's cheek, making a flat sickening sound.

The man staggered back against the wall again, and still did not go down. And suddenly, Hawker was back in the old Bridgeport Gym in Chicago again; back training for the Golden Gloves championship, light heavyweight class, and this stranger was the heavy bag.

Hawker pummeled his ribs and belly, then raised his shots higher when the man's arms fell limply to his sides. Hawker's left hand held the man by the throat as he drove his right fist home again and again and again until, suddenly, there was someone beside him, pulling at him, and there was a voice:

"James! *James!* It's over, for God's sake!"

Hawker stepped back dizzily, and the man slithered down the wall, collapsing at his feet.

Barbara Blaine was at his elbow. Hawker took a deep breath and shook himself out of the dreamy world of near-unconsciousness. He took her by the arms suddenly. "Are you all right?"

"Yes . . . I think so. He knocked the wind out of me for a second, I guess. When I finally got to my feet, you were beating him. You beat him for a long time. It seemed like you would never quit. That's why I got up. That's why I stopped you."

Hawker wiped his hand over his face, checking for blood. Amazingly, there was none. He hadn't been shot, yet his left ear still burned. The man had fired the gun so close that the powder detonation had scorched him.

Hawker kneeled over the man. He was bigger than he had expected. Six-three or six-four, maybe 260 pounds. Black, carefully oiled hair over the pulpy mass of face. Dark long-sleeved shirt and dark slacks. Clothes for night stealth. Hawker touched his fingers to the man's neck, then stood.

"He's dead."

The woman put her hands to her face. "My God, this is awful, James." She hesitated. "The police—I'd better go call them."

Hawker turned from her and began searching in the bushes where he had first collided with the man. "That's a decision you'll have to make, Barbara. We have every right to defend your property—but that's not going to make the publicity any better. Personally, I have a real aversion to seeing my name in print."

"But we have to do something, James. We just can't leave him here."

Hawker kneeled and carefully listened to the shoebox-size package the man had been carrying. In the weak light that came through the main window, he could see that the box was built of wood and metal. There was a toggle switch on the wooden frame and a kitchen timer.

A homemade bomb.

Hawker wondered if he should tell the woman. He decided not to. No sense upsetting her any more than she was.

He stood. "'We' don't have to do anything, Barbara. Right now I want you to go inside. Don't tell any of the girls, because it will just upset them. But first, I want to make sure you don't need any medical attention."

She shook her head. "I don't think so. Like I said, I just had the wind knocked out of me."

"Good. Then go back inside. Get your car keys for me. Then, if you're able, go to the front of the house and join the party. It'll take your mind off what I'm doing."

"Are you sure I shouldn't go with you? You might need some help. You've been badly hurt, James."

"Just bring me your car keys, Barbara. And leave me alone."

There was a wistful tone in her voice. "You'll stop back . . . later? It doesn't matter how late. God, after tonight, I don't think I could get to sleep no matter what."

Hawker squeezed the woman's arm gently. "I'll be back, Barbara. I promise."

TEN

Two hours later, just before midnight, Hawker pulled into the parking lot of the Doll House. He steered the car around back, touched the Genie control and the garage door slid open. He got out of the car and closed the garage door behind him.

It was a full-size American car. Black metallic paint and a lot of useless electronic gadgets guaranteed to drive the average mechanic right out of his mind. But the car had a trunk bigger than the wheelbase of most of the Jap imports.

Hawker had hooked up the sweeper before he left. He vacuumed the trunk thoroughly, then vacuumed his own clothes. Then he carried the catch bag to a stainless steel sink mounted inside the garage and flushed the contents down. Then he shoved the catch bag deep into the garbage.

A professional job. And getting rid of the body is always the trickiest part.

Even trickier than disconnecting the dry cell from a home-made bomb.

Hawker knew too well that a murderer could be traced by

a microscopic speck of thread in the suspect's trunk, which was exactly why he had blanketed the trunk with garbage bags before dumping the corpse in.

Vacuuming the car had been an added precaution.

As he double-checked the car's interior, Hawker found his memory drifting back to the *ker-chunk* of his shovel cutting the night silence; the image of him draping the corpse over his shoulder and walking heavily beneath the star-bowl of desert darkness; the remembrance of the gaseous hiss and fecal stink as he dumped the corpse into that infinite pit which, he knew, would inevitably swallow him and all other temporal creatures who reared themselves on two legs to walk the earth as gods— for their pathetically short threescore and ten.

Death adds an edge to reality. It throws a damp gray gauze over the spirit.

James Hawker wearily rotated his head on his neck.

He turned the knob to Barbara Blaine's suite and wasn't surprised to find it locked.

He was almost glad.

In him there was no longer a taste for feminine company and polite conversation.

He wanted to be alone for a while; away from the humid looks and the wilting perfume and the teary-eyed gazes.

He was eager to get back to his room at the Mirage. Eager to wash the night away with a hot shower, crack a cold beer and get to work. He wanted to check his room for electronic listening devices, and he had to get moving on breaking the code Jason Stratton had used in his journal. He also had to talk with Captain Kevin Smith at greater length, and maybe get a hook on who—if anyone—in Smith's employ was spying for the mob.

But as he turned to go, the door opened. Barbara Blaine stood before him. She wore a white satin pajama suit. The high collar gave it an oriental flavor. Her black hair was longer than he had thought, combed in a dark sheen over her shoulders. Her brown eyes were a combination of worry and hurt.

"You were leaving?"

"Yeah."

"Did . . . everything go all right?"

"Just peachy. He wasn't carrying any identification, so I didn't learn anything about him. And his car—if he came by car—wasn't parked anyplace obvious. Strike two."

"I know you're upset, James. But you don't have to turn your sarcasm against me."

He made an impatient gesture with his hands. "I guess I'm just in no mood for interrogation, Barbara."

"Is that what I was doing?"

Hawker punched a button on the wall, and the garage door rolled open. He said over his shoulder, "I'll call you tomorrow, Barbara."

Her voice turned chilly. "If it's really necessary, James."

He thought of a number of cutting replies, most of them dealing with how many times it had been necessary for him to call a whorehouse. But he choked down the surge of adolescent meanness and walked silently into the darkness as the door clattered down behind him.

Hawker was a hundred yards down the road when he heard the *clumpity-pat* of her slippers on the pavement. He turned and saw her running toward him, running with that peculiar stride of the dancer—hands too low, legs too straight.

Her eyes glistened in the streetlights. Hawker did not respond when she threw her arms around him, crying.

"Oh, Hawk, there was no reason for saying what I did. It was cruel of me—especially after what you had to do tonight."

Hawker patted her shoulder noncommittally. "It's okay, Barbara. Really. I'm just tired. I need to get some sleep."

He tried to pull away from her, but she wouldn't allow it. "No. You're still mad. And besides, you're tight as a drum. I can feel it in your shoulders. They're all knotted. You won't be able to sleep even if you try." She took his big hand and tugged him back toward the Doll House. "I owe you a dinner and an apology. And if you go off and leave me feeling the way I do, James Hawker, I really never will speak to you again."

So, feeling sheepish and silly, Hawker allowed himself to be led back to the suite; allowed her to hum and cluck over him while a striking blonde served them roast quail and wild rice and fresh strawberries and a French wine so good that he actually drank two glasses before ordering the beer he had wanted so badly.

And when he stood to thank her for the meal, Barbara Blaine took his hand once again and pulled him along behind her. She took him out onto the patio and into a small adjoining building. The structure smelled of cedar and heat.

The tiny room in which they stood was tiled from wall to ceiling, and there was a stainless steel table near the shower stall. "That," said the woman, pointing toward a large window through which Hawker could see cedar benches, "is the sauna bath. The girls have had it on most of the night, so the temperature should be about one-seventy. Right outside is a Jacuzzi. We keep it at about one-ten. You need to relax, and *those* two will relax you." She pointed to the table. "That is for massages. One of my girls is an accredited masseuse, and I will send her down in about half an hour—"

"Barbara, that's really not necessary—"

"Not a word, James Hawker. You're going to have a proper massage, whether you like it or not. Her name is Mary Kay O'Mordecai Flynn, and Mary Kay O'Mordecai Flynn is also going to bandage your cuts and soothe your wounds, and make you feel altogether human again—"

"I think I've already turned down that offer—"

"A *massage*, James, and some tender loving care—nothing more. I will send down a girl immediately with a bucket of ice. In that bucket of ice, you will find a fresh bottle of beer. Drink the beer and then soak those awful knuckles of yours in the ice. Every twenty minutes thereafter, I will send another beer and another bucket." She stood to her full height, fists perched on her hips. It was the first real smile Hawker had seen on her haunting Mediterranean face, and he realized that she was really enjoying this opportunity to please him.

He smiled. "You really are something, Barbara Blaine."

She stuck out her small hand. "Friends again?"

"Friends."

Mary Kay O'Mordecai Flynn had flaming red hair, the body of a centerfold, the face of a country saint, the personality of a Midwestern homecoming queen, and the finger strength of a professional wrestler.

Hawker had sweated himself in the sauna, soaked himself in the Jacuzzi and dutifully drunk the three prescribed beers. Now he lay naked on the table with a towel thrown over his hips. Even if he had had the energy to move, he wouldn't have.

Mary Kay O'Mordecai Flynn wore a lime-colored body stocking cut low enough at the bosom to show the healthy swell of tanned cleavage; cut high enough at her hips to display the long, lithe thighs and the indentation of partially bared buttocks.

She didn't massage Hawker's muscles, she attacked them, pushing and pulling and kneading as if there were evil creatures inside him that damn well needed exorcising.

"Does this hurt, Mr. Hawker?"

"Arrrrg . . ."

"Does this hurt, Mr. Hawker?"

"Oooooh . . ."

"Does *this* hurt, Mr. Hawker?"

"Oh, lordy . . ."

"Is there any place on your body that doesn't hurt, Mr. Hawker?"

"Only one spot, Mary Kay, but you keep those meathooks of yours away from it!"

But soon the pain melted away, replaced by a bone-deep relaxation that Hawker had not experienced for a very long time. The girl rolled him over on his back and began to work on his chest and stomach muscles.

Her breasts hung temptingly over his face, and Hawker found it easier to endure if he closed his eyes.

Soon he was asleep.

He awoke in the midst of a dream. In the dream, Mary

Kay O'Mordecai Flynn had begun taking liberties beneath the towel. In the dream, Hawker reacted the way most healthy men would react . . .

But then his eyes fluttered open, and he felt the woman's lips on him; could smell the light scent of the unfamiliar perfume—a wry, delicate musk; could feel her body tremble when he reached out and cupped the heavy, naked breast in his right hand.

"Mary Kay?"

The door was closed, and the room was a void of darkness.

The woman did not answer.

"Mary Kay? Is that you?"

Still holding him in her small warm hand, the woman kissed her way up his chest to his lips, as if to silence him. Hawker slid off the table, too engulfed by the dreamy reality to question or moralize. He spread towels on the floor with his foot, then pulled the woman down with him, touching the softness of her face with his fingertips, then tracing the firm line of her body; tracing the curvature of ribs and the soft swell of thighs and the satin curl of vaginal hair.

Since he could not see her with his eyes, he had to look at her with his fingers.

Once again she found him with her lips as Hawker kneeled over her. When he could stand it no more, he set his tongue to work on her, massaging the delicate folds until she moaned and trembled and heaved.

He entered her then; rolled her over on top of him, and entered from beneath, as the woman's hips began the timeless lift, arc and fall of the final coupling.

There seemed to be a fever in her body, a searing skin temperature that increased as the rhythm of their joining gained momentum.

It was a strange pairing. Hawker had no idea who his partner was, yet there was an unexpected tenderness in their loving and an inexplicable charge of emotion.

As the woman reached her climax, her lips betrayed a muffled cry as she clawed at Hawker, burying her face in the hair on his chest.

It was the first time he had heard her voice, yet it was too distorted to tell him whom he had just made love with.

Hawker tried to speak, but once again the woman covered his lips with her hands. They dozed for a while, then made love again—this time each making sure it lasted a long, long time for the other.

When Hawker awoke again, a thin line of light filtered beneath the massage room door.

It was morning.

And the woman was gone.

ELEVEN

Hawker spent the next morning, a Thursday morning, sleeping.

He had wandered away from the Doll House at dawn, too tired to explain his leaving or to say good-bye.

It didn't appear anyone was up anyway.

Back in his own suite, he opened the windows, turned the air-conditioning on high and tumbled into bed.

He awoke four hours later to the sound of laughter. It was 11:35 A.M., and the showgirls were beneath his veranda again, sunning themselves at the pool.

The long-legged beauty with the tawny red hair was there. Her bikini was wet, and Hawker could see the outline of upturned nipples through the thin material.

As though she could feel Hawker's eyes on her, the woman turned suddenly and caught him in his act of voyeurism.

Hawker hadn't blushed in a very long time, but he came damn close now. The woman seemed to sense it and grinned at him. Then, with a toss of her auburn mane, she dove headlong into the pool. Hawker felt the urge to slip on his swimsuit and trot downstairs for the obligatory inanities of introduction.

It would be nice to escape from the dangers of this mission for a while.

Hawker watched the auburn-haired girl swim. Her stroke was long and effective but surprisingly lacking in grace. Her buttocks pivoted alluringly with every kick, and the stirring he felt reminded him of the mystery woman who had come to him in the darkness. Who was she? Barbara Blaine? Mary Kay O'Mordecai Flynn? Or just one of the anonymous girls, a prostitute who had come to him with inexplicable desire?

It was a pleasant mystery, and Hawker used it to take his mind off the girl in the pool.

But then he cursed himself for mooning around like a love-struck adolescent. He had work to do, damn it. Important work. He had had enough of women for the time being.

Hawker ordered breakfast from room service, then forced himself beneath a cold shower.

After the fight he had had, he expected to feel more soreness. Instead, he felt pretty good—except for the knuckles of his right hand.

The massage had apparently helped.

Hawker dressed himself in worn twill slacks, a black cotton knit shirt and a pair of waxy soft boat shoes. He had already inventoried the armaments in the carefully packed crates, so it didn't take him long to find what he was looking for.

It was a VL-34, brand named the Privacy Protector. It was built of red plastic, and considerably smaller than a paperback book. The VL-34 was the smallest and most advanced electronic bug-detecting device ever built.

Hawker checked the batteries and drew out the retractable antenna. He pointed the antenna toward the television set. The little beeper alarm went off immediately, but the tiny fail-safe yellow flasher did not come on.

No bugs there.

Hawker went over the entire suite painstakingly. And found nothing.

It was not good news. It meant there were now only three ways the mob could have found out about his plans to drive to Jason Stratton's cabin: through a spy among Kevin Smith's help, through Barbara Blaine or through a wiretap.

The wiretap would be the easiest to check, and Hawker decided to take care of that after breakfast.

But while waiting for his food to arrive, he pulled out Stratton's cryptic journal and went through it carefully.

Aside from a few seemingly unimportant entries, the only things Stratton had not written in code were the dates of his entries.

He had been keeping the journal for just over two years. The entries had been made sporadically over that time period, sometimes weekly, sometimes daily.

The last three entries were dated June 9, June 10 and June 13.

Barbara Blaine said Jason had disappeared in mid-June.

Hawker found a tablet and pen and sat at the desk with the journal. On the tablet he wrote:

E-T-O-N-A-I

These were the most often used letters in the English language. Beneath them he wrote:

R-S-H-D-L-C-W-U-M

These were the second most often used letters. Then he printed the rest of the alphabet in the order of the letters' respective usage:

F-Y-G-P-B-V-K-X-Q-J-Z

That done, Hawker studied Stratton's journal carefully. He looked for some immediate solution but found none. He couldn't break the code into distinct words, spaces and punctuation. Some of Stratton's sentences consisted of more than a thousand unspaced letters and numbers in a row.

But Barbara had said he had invented the code when he was a teenager. It couldn't be too complicated.

Hawker hoped.

He sat hunched over the desk for more than two hours. The wastebasket beside the desk slowly filled. At a quarter of one, Hawker decided Jason Stratton had been a very precocious teenager. At two P.M., Hawker decided the CIA had missed a good bet in not recruiting the young Stratton and putting him in charge of its covert operations section.

He had made very little headway with the code. Very little. There was some definite correlation between the numbers that intermixed with the rows of letters. But Hawker couldn't quite put his finger on it. It seemed just out of reach.

By two thirty his eyes were tired and he realized the breakfast he had ordered from room service had still not arrived.

Hawker found another Walther PPK in the armaments crate, pulled on a sports jacket and went outside into the corridor. After locking the door behind him, he tugged out a few strands of hair and wet them with saliva, then pasted them across the crack in the door.

He had already had enough surprises in Las Vegas.

He had given the mob two easy chances to kill him, and he wasn't about to give them a third.

TWELVE

After grabbing a sandwich in the restaurant, Hawker found Kevin Smith in his office. A big, comfortable office of wood and glass and leather, for a stocky, comfortable man.

Smith still looked more like a cop than a casino operator. Like a cross between Lou Grant and Rocky Marciano. Smith was in his early sixties. He was only a few inches under six feet tall, but his barrel chest and thick forearms made him look shorter. The graying hair was sparse enough to show a well-tanned head beneath. The face was full and jowly, and his small blue eyes crinkled when he smiled—and he smiled often.

He listened intently as Hawker briefed him on his two clashes with the mob. When Hawker had finished, Smith tapped a pencil on his desk impatiently.

"The bastards," he said in soft exclamation. "It just doesn't make any sense." He thought for a moment, then reconsidered. "Well, maybe it does."

Hawker sat across from him in a heavy leather chair. The

leather creaked whenever he shifted his weight. "What do you mean, Kevin?"

Smith shrugged noncommittally. "I'm not sure, really, Hawk. But maybe I've underestimated the worth of the Five-Cs. I know the mob operates in Vegas. Hell, what cop doesn't? But they aren't nearly as strong as they were, say, thirty years ago. When the big legitimate conglomerates began to hear what kind of profits a casino made, they started buying out the mob. Howard Hughes paved the way." Smith smiled. "Not even the mob could turn down dough like that."

"What's that have to do with the Five-Cs?"

Smith hunched forward to make his point. "It's this, Hawk. The mob has slowly been losing control. But the things they have held on to have been solid—either established casinos or a few selected outside businesses. Their outside businesses have nothing to do with gambling, but it gives them a place to wash any illegal money they have. We started the Five-Cs six years ago. We started small. Hell, we *wanted* to be small. That way, the outsiders wouldn't be interested. Why would the mob want to bother with us? But our casinos are like no others in Vegas. They're individualized. Very personal. I've been told they have kind of a hometown flavor. And maybe that's why our success has been three times what we ever hoped it would be."

"You're making a lot of money?"

Smith nodded quickly, as if he couldn't believe it himself. "Not compared to a really big casino. But we're still making more than I ever dreamed. And maybe the mob found out. I mean, that *has* to be it, doesn't it? Why else would they want a gambling complex? Maybe they decided the Five-Cs is the place to get their foot back in the door. Maybe they're making another run at Vegas so they can get the same kind of control they had in the old days." He stared out the window. "God knows, their methods are the same as in the old days. Extortion. Threats. Murder."

"You said the mob still controls some businesses that have nothing to do with gambling. What kind?"

"I don't know for sure, really. It's just talk I've heard. A chain of carpet cleaner outlets. Liquor stores." He grinned. "A religious supply company."

"What?"

"You heard me right. Las Vegas has more churches than any city its size in the world, Hawk. And it's not accidental. You see, the good citizens of this state can outlaw gambling anytime they want—at the voting booth. The mob and other casino owners have always been painfully aware of that. So to keep the citizens happy, they give them anything they want. And because most of the antigambling sentiment comes from the churchgoers, people in the business have taken special care to make them happy. Twenty years ago, if a congregation wanted a new church, all they had to do was drop the word to the mob boss. Presto! The money magically arrived. Name any religious sect and I'll guarantee they have a place of worship here. And it probably didn't cost the happy flock a dime."

"The mob bought off ministers?"

"And rabbis and priests and yogis and everyone else you can think of." Smith laced his fingers behind his head and rocked back in his chair. "So you see, running a religious supply store is a way for the mob to get some of its money back. Clever, huh?"

"Touching."

"The mob has always had a heart of gold. Believe me, I know. I've been in Vegas for more than forty years."

"And that's one thing that bothers me, Kevin. You were a cop here. A damn good cop, from what I've heard. And all good cops make street connections—people who can tell them what the opposition is up to."

Smith nodded that it was true.

Hawker looked at him pointedly. "So how is it you people don't know who is trying to hit you? Certainly the word is out on the streets. But from what you've said, they came to you out of the blue. Two goons you had never seen before tendering a low-ball offer for your complex. When you refused them, the telephone threats began—just as they threatened Barbara Blaine. And then a couple of them jumped your associate, Charlie Kullenburg, and beat him half to death. And you still don't have a clue who they are."

Smith's face reddened slightly. "Goddamn it, Hawk, don't you think I've tried? Don't you think we've all tried? I agree, it's confusing as hell. It doesn't make any sense. But who else could it be but the old Vegas mob? Sure, the word should be on the streets—but it's not. People on the in with the old mob families should know why they want the Five-Cs and just how far they're willing to go to get it—but they don't. I can't explain it. It's one hell of a mystery.

"When it first started, I wasn't worried a bit. I was confident there wasn't anything the five of us couldn't handle—we're all cops, for Christ's sake. And we've still got connections downtown." He made a helpless motion with his hands. "But things have changed more than I thought in Vegas. It used to be I *knew* who the mob bosses were. I could recognize their goons a hundred yards away. But like I said, the big conglomerate money has shifted the center of power. The mob is still here. But they don't run the place anymore, so who keeps up with them?"

"And that includes the Vegas police?"

"To a certain extent. Hell, that's why I knew we had to bring in an outsider. Even my cop friends can't find out anything. They have to play everything exactly by the book. And until these bastards come out in the open, they can't even hit them with a loitering charge." Kevin Smith stood suddenly, smiling as if his good humor had returned. "But that's enough talk about those bums for now, Hawk. I haven't even given you a tour of the casino yet."

"Can you include a visit to your switchboard terminal station in the tour?"

Smith looked at him oddly. "Sure. If you want."

"I want."

Even though it was a Thursday afternoon, the casino was crowded.

The noise of a jazzy band from one of the lounge areas mixed with the alto garble of crowd noise. Men in white dinner jackets. Middle-aged women in gowns designed to reveal rather than conceal. Cigarette smoke and wild peals of laughter.

Hawker didn't like crowds. He decided it was to be one of those tours that had to be politely endured.

He was wrong.

Kevin Smith knew the casino business, and Hawker soon found himself fascinated by the intricacies of managing a big-time gambling operation. Smith led him through the rows of slot machines in the lobby, all attended by handle-yanking women, purses on their laps.

"There're more than sixty thousand slots in Nevada," Smith said, raising his voice above the noise of the crowd. "I think I already told you the kind of revenue they produce. It's because people get addicted to the little bastards. Hell, they're always trying to beat them one way or another. They try foreign coins, wire shims, kicking and punching them—it must have something to do with people hating to lose to machines. We went through a period when ladies were bringing big magnets to throw off the mechanism. They'd carry the magnets in their purses and hold them up to the window to stop the wheels. Christ, one night we caught a lady in here with a magnet that must have weighed forty pounds—carried the damn thing in a purse the size of a suitcase. When we asked her how she'd managed, she told us in absolute seriousness, 'Practice.' Turns out she'd ripped off just about every casino in Vegas. And the old dame was proud of herself!"

The women at the slot machines did not glance up as the two men pressed by.

The main casino was ballroom-sized. The balcony was right out of a Western movie. The gambling tables were the color of fine putting greens. The roulette wheels took center stage, spinning and clattering as the players watched, mesmerized.

To Hawker, it was a blur of random activity. But Smith began to bring it all into focus.

"Hawk, a casino manager has to win his money three times here. First I have to win it from the players. Then from the dealers. Then from my behind-the-scenes people."

"Am I supposed to understand that, Kevin?"

The older man laughed. "Stealing, Hawk. Greed. I employ good people here. But it's an awful damn big temptation to handle all those high-stake chips every night without trying to pocket one or two. In Vegas, you see, a casino chip is as good as cash. So to combat that, I use the same system most of the casinos use. For each eight-hour shift, I have a shift boss. He's the overseer. He runs the show. Under him, we have pit bosses. There's a pit boss for the blackjack pit, where all the blackjack tables are; a pit boss for the dice pit, one for the baccarat tables; and so on. The pit bosses are in charge of all the tables in their area—a big responsibility with all the noise and activity going on. So to help them, we have floor men who walk up and down behind the dealers to make sure no one gets lighthanded. At the baccarat tables, we have a ladder man—a guy who sits on a stand and watches from above . . ."

As Smith talked, all the random activity came into focus for Hawker. The strategic placement of the employees, he realized, was as carefully planned as the location of teller windows at banks.

What Hawker found especially interesting was the way Smith said the casinos dealt with gamblers who owed them money.

"All casinos have a marker system, Hawk. That means we will extend the customer credit if he signs a marker for it. Sometimes customers skip when it comes time to collect. Every year, the Five-Cs complex extends about a million in credit, and we usually fail to collect about two hundred thousand. So we send out our collectors. In the movies, our collectors would be Humphrey Bogart types. You know, tough guys. They'd break legs, threaten wives, whatever it took to get the money." Smith laughed. "But it's nothing like that. You see, a gambling debt cannot be legally collected. And there isn't a casino manager or stockholder who doesn't want it to stay that way."

"What?"

"I'm serious. Making gambling debts legally collectible would be the beginning of the end of our business. Think about it. A day wouldn't go by that a newspaper didn't carry the story of how some local family man had lost everything to a Vegas gambling casino. Very bad for the image, and the voters don't like that sort of thing. Plus, ruining an avid gambler is strictly a stupid thing to do. Even if he does owe you money, he's going to keep working and keep gambling as long as he's not in prison—which he would be, if we had to take our debtors to court. You see, Hawk, a casino owner looks upon each avid gambler as an annuity. A gambler pays steady dividends over the years. And we'll go way out of our way to make sure he doesn't get hurt too badly on a trip to one of our casinos. We want to keep him healthy. We want to keep him working."

"But why would you have to collect? Even if the debt was legally collectible, why would you have to pursue it?"

"Because the IRS would make us. The IRS is the only one that wants to make gambling debts legally collectible. That way they can tax the money twice. You see, when a debtor welches on us, we don't have to pay taxes on it because it's money we never received. It goes down as a business loss. So the IRS says we have to make a 'reasonable' effort to collect. So we send out collectors. If the gambler tells the collector to get the hell off his property, the collector gets in his car and comes home. We've made our reasonable effort. And our gambler is still healthy and working. When he's feeling lucky, he'll return to our casinos and place a few bets. Of course, the IRS is pissed off, but what else is new?"

Kevin Smith spent another hour showing Hawker the casino. The terminology was new but interesting. Hawker learned about shills, drop boxes, croupiers and crossroaders.

It was while he was at the roulette table that the key to Jason Stratton's code finally came to Hawker.

Kevin Smith was explaining how the random probabilities aren't always so random in roulette.

"Big-time gamblers have hired scientists to make studies," Smith was saying. "See, all the numbers on the wheel are either red or black. These scientists discovered that red paint and black paint have different chemical properties. Black paint tends to make the wooden fibers of the wheel harder, and thus helps the ball to bounce out. But red paint eats into the wooden fibers of the slot and helps the ball stick. The difference in the percentages is small, but I've read there is some truth to it . . ."

Hawker didn't hear the rest of what he was saying. Something he had said kept echoing in his head. ". . . the random probabilities aren't always so random."

Now excited about finally getting into Stratton's journal, Hawker cut the tour short. Kevin Smith insisted on going with him to the switchboard terminal. It was downstairs in the guts of the building, amid boxes of musty show costumes, retired slot machines, roulette wheels.

The terminal station had a room all its own. On each wall was a closet-size beige terminal box. Inside each box was a vein-work of candy-colored wires running to rows of clattering switching stations.

Hawker brought out the VL-34 and drew out the antenna. With all the electrical equipment around, the audio alert went off immediately. But it wasn't until he pointed the antenna at the second bank of switches that the flashing yellow light told him there was an in-house tap.

It took Hawker all of thirty seconds to find the mouse-size bug.

Captain Kevin Smith looked on, beaming his approval as Hawker held up his find.

But then the door to the terminal flew open, and a man dressed in coveralls stepped in.

The stocking knotted over his head contorted his face into a fleshy mass.

The .45 automatic in his right hand was up and firing before Hawker could react.

There were two deafening explosions, and Kevin Smith was smacked back against the wall.

Hawker was already in mid-stride as the .45's muzzle vectored toward him.

THIRTEEN

Hawker stepped under the gun, then locked both hands on the man's arm. He slammed downward, as if trying to break firewood over his knee.

The man in the stocking mask screamed in agony as the gun fell to the cement floor.

There was an explosion. For a crazy moment, Hawker thought Kevin Smith had somehow found a weapon and fired. The man in the stocking mask jolted backward, blood spouting from beneath his chin.

It took Hawker a second to realize what had happened.

The impact of the .45 hitting the cement had triggered it.

The man had been killed by his own weapon.

Hawker had been holding him by the bib of his coveralls. The accidental shot had come all too close. Hawker released his grip, and the man fell heavily to the floor. His hand moved sleepily to the black hole in his throat.

Hawker rushed to the fallen Captain Smith. He was still conscious, but bleeding from the shoulder.

Smith winced as Hawker forced him to lie flat on his back. Because there was nothing else available, Hawker dragged the corpse of their attacker over and used it to elevate Smith's feet.

More gunshot victims die because of shock than because of the slugs in them.

"How bad is it?" Smith demanded. "Where did he get me?"

"The shoulder. He shot twice, but I think one of them went into the wall."

"Shit, it feels like Nolan Ryan hit me with a brick from about five feet away." He chuckled through the sweat and pain. "All those years on the force, and I never even got a scratch. This is a real pisser, Hawk."

"You're going to be okay, Kev. Just hold tight. I'm going to get help."

As Hawker turned to go, Smith called after him. "Hawk! I want you to nail these bastards, Hawk. I want you to make them wish they had never been born."

Hawker winked at him. "Forty-eight hours, Captain. If things go right, it should all be over in forty-eight hours."

So Hawker made his way through the throng of gamblers as fast as he could without causing panic. He buttonholed the same deskman from the day before.

When Hawker told him Kevin Smith had been shot, the deskman's European facade fell away like a cheap suit. His eyes bulged as he dialed the emergency number. He screamed for an ambulance in a rank Bronx accent.

Hawker carried a blanket and a flagon of water back to the basement. Smith was in pain but resting when the men with the stretcher got there. The EMTs agreed the wound wasn't too bad. Smith would be okay.

And then the police came, and Hawker had to keep repeating his story. Policemen ask a great deal of questions when there is a corpse involved. Hawker did his best to seem naive, helpful and polite.

"No, Officer, I have no idea who the man was and why he might want to shoot Captain Smith. Hell, this is my first trip to Vegas. Captain Smith was just showing me around. Yes, Officer, I was so scared I guess I kind of got woozy and fell toward the guy. I must have hit his hand or something, because his gun dropped to the floor and went off. What? No, the guy never said a word after he fell. But frankly, I wasn't doing much listening. All that blood and excitement. I think I must have passed out for a second. Next thing I knew, the guy in the stocking mask was dead, and Captain Smith was telling me to go get help. No, Officer, he didn't say a word to us. At least, I don't *think* he did. Captain Smith could probably tell you better. He was a policeman, so he's probably used to this kind of excitement. Personally, if I never hear another gun go off in my life, I'll be happy. I still feel kind of dizzy. Like I might faint or something."

The John Q. Public act worked, and the police dismissed Hawker quickly. They had enough on their minds without having to worry about some tourist with a bad case of the faints.

Hawker didn't waste any time getting back to his room. After first making sure the strands of hair were still safely in place at the front door, Hawker entered, slipped his shoes and jacket off, grabbed a cold beer from the refrigerator and carried Jason Stratton's journal to the desk.

The problem he had had with the journal was that he couldn't segment the seemingly random letters into word blocks. All the letters ran together with an occasional number thrown in. Some of the numbers had up to four digits.

A sentence might read:

S73hbr3521usra9lXzwxzwz....

The use of the numbers was the most confusing thing. Hawker had at first assumed they filled their obvious role. Stratton was a scientist, and scientists use a lot of numbers.

But then Hawker saw that there were numbers throughout the entries. Far too many numbers to be anything but part of the code.

And that was what had stumped him.

But when Kevin Smith had said the random numbers in roulette weren't always so random, it crossed Hawker's mind that Stratton's journal might benefit from the same paradox. The random numbers *weren't* random.

It took Hawker an intense two hours to crack the code. And when he finally got the key, he cursed himself for not recognizing the simplicity of it. Stratton had invented it as a teenager, after all. It had to be reasonably basic. And it was. But Stratton had been smart enough to use numbers to camouflage it, make it seem harder than it was.

Stratton had invented the code to protect his most private thoughts from the prying eyes of outsiders. Later, as an adult, he had used it out of habit, secure, perhaps, in the knowledge that someone else in his field would find it difficult to plagiarize his observations.

Hawker concentrated on decoding the last three entries. He stopped only to dial the front desk and demand that a typewriter be sent to his room immediately.

Probably because of the tone of Hawker's voice, room service was uncharacteristically efficient. The typewriter arrived ten minutes later.

It was a simple surrogate code, taken from the arrangement of a typewriter keyboard. Z had replaced A, X had replaced B and so on. All the numbers did was denote spaces between the words. They had no other meaning. And were chosen completely at random. Numbers that actually belonged within the context of the sentence were enclosed in brackets.

Slowly, the last three entries began to reveal themselves.

There were a few touching references to Barbara Blaine. His lover; his wife to be. But the entries largely concerned a discovery he had made. A wonderful discovery, in the mind of Jason Stratton.

A discovery that would make it possible for Barbara to give up her business. A discovery that would bring them enough money to get married and live happily ever after. The discovery all keyed around a word Hawker didn't recognize.

The word was *pitchblende*.

At first, Hawker thought the word was just more of Stratton's code talk. But on a hunch, he called room service again, and in the same dire tone, demanded that the necessary reference book be sent up immediately.

The book took twenty-five minutes.

It was worth the wait.

Jason Stratton had made an interesting discovery, all right.

Pitchblende.

But it was a discovery that had, in fact, sentenced him to death.

As Hawker labored over the journal, he began to feel as if he had known Jason Stratton. And he liked him. Stratton had the brain of a scientist but the heart of a man-child.

The innocence Barbara Blaine had mentioned permeated the journal. Stratton wrote with wonder and joy and humor. And Hawker felt himself feeling very damn bad that they had never had the chance to meet.

Hawker could picture Stratton as a shy teenager, hunched over the typewriter keys as he invented his secret code, grinning at his own cunning, delighted that he had finally figured out how to fool the intimidating adults in his world.

Later, the code would be used to record such esoteric findings as sedimentary clastic deposits in an ancient riverbed.

Hawker wondered how Stratton would have reacted if he could have known his code would someday make it possible to take revenge on his killers.

FOURTEEN

Hawker got the name of the corporation from Stratton's journal.

He got the address from telephone information, but the address meant nothing to him.

Rural Route #7, Pahrump, Nevada.

Where in the hell was Pahrump, Nevada?

He decided Barbara Blaine might be able to help. He picked up the phone to call her, then reasoned it might be better to see her face to face. Making love with an unidentified woman in pitch darkness can, after a time, become a disruptive influence on the powers of ratiocination.

Hawker wanted a clear mind for the work ahead. Besides, he was growing anxious as hell to find out whom he had slept with the previous night.

He telephoned downstairs to the deskman. The deskman had recovered his composure and his European accent. After being reassured that Kevin Smith had been transported to the hospital and was in good condition, Hawker asked that a car be sent around for his use.

As he stepped outside, he saw the bellboy dangling the keys to the Jaguar in his hand. Hawker took them wordlessly and slid in behind the wheel. The bullet hole in the windshield had been fixed, no questions asked. But it did explain the wicked grin on the bellboy's face.

Hawker drove the short distance to the Doll House.

It was late afternoon, and the three-story house looked white and clean in the desert sunlight.

He considered going around back to Barbara's suite, but he decided that in the event he was being tailed, going to the front door might be more appropriate.

Mary Kay O'Mordecai Flynn answered the Big Ben gongs. She wore white shorts and a lime green blouse that brought out the color of her eyes. Her face was even more striking than he remembered, and she looked as fresh as if she had slept fourteen sound hours.

Her greeting was warm, but communicated nothing. Her handshake was brief and offered no conspiratorial squeeze.

"How are you feeling, Mr. Hawker?"

"Great, thanks to that massage you gave me, Mary Kay." Hawker watched her eyes closely. "It felt so good, I must have drifted off to sleep, huh?"

The woman laughed. "You sure did! You must have a pretty good pain tolerance, Mr. Hawker, because I was really working on you."

"Oh? How much longer after I fell asleep?"

"Not long. Ten minutes, maybe. I had to cut it short because I had to get to bed. I've got company staying with me here and I had to get up early for breakfast. I was a tour guide most of the morning."

That seemed to put an end to all speculation about Mary Kay O'Mordecai Flynn. She led him through the main sitting room. Some of the girls he recognized from the night before were now listening to the jukebox and playing cards. They smiled warmly and waved at him.

Barbara Blaine was in her den, doing paperwork. She stood up quickly when Hawker entered. Her face was pale, and she looked shaken.

"My God, James, I just heard the news about Captain Smith. It was on the radio. I called the hospital, but they wouldn't give out any details. Then I tried to call you, but you had just left—"

Hawker took her by the elbows. "Relax, Barbara. He's okay. Kevin's just fine."

"Damnit, Hawk, isn't there any way to stop those bastards!" She turned away from him and walked to the window.

"There is now, Barbara. I've read Jason's journal."

She turned quickly. "His journal? You figured it out? You broke the code?"

"Yeah. And it's all in there. I know why they want your property and the Five-Cs complex. And I know why they're willing to kill for it."

"Then tell me, for Christ's sake. Tell me what could be worth all this misery."

Hawker reached into his coat pocket and extracted the journal. He handed it to the woman. "You'll want to read it yourself, Barbara. I put the key to the code inside the jacket. You won't have any trouble with it. I didn't read it all. I didn't have time and, besides, I suspect it's too personal. He mentions you often."

She took the black book. Her eyes glistened. "Oh, James, I'm so, so sorry he's gone."

"Me, too, Barbara. Especially after reading his journal. He was one of the rare ones. One of the good ones. We can't afford to lose our Jason Strattons." Hawker cupped his hand behind the woman's head and kissed her gently on the nose. "Can you answer a few questions, lady?"

She sniffed and pawed at her eyes with a small fist. "Sure, Hawk. Damn, you must think I'm a regular waterworks. Every time you see me I'm crying."

"Don't worry about it. I can't bring Jason back, but I think I can solve your problems with the mob."

"Then it is the mob?"

"Yes. In a way. Barbara, did Jason ever mention a corporation called Nevada Mining and Assay?"

The woman touched her finger to her lips as she concentrated. "No-o-o-o. No, I don't think so. Is it important?"

"You might say that. I can get the information somewhere else if you don't know. But I was hoping Jason might have mentioned the name of someone he dealt with there. It would help."

"Jason did most of his own chemical analysis. He seemed very proficient. He liked that sort of thing, working over his little Bunsen burner with chemicals and stuff. But he did mention that he was having trouble with one of his projects. He didn't say what exactly, but he did say he lacked the equipment to do a proper job."

Hawker nodded. "I know. It was in the journal. Barbara, do you know where Pahrump, Nevada, is?"

"Sure. I know because Jason and I drove through there once

on the way to Death Valley. Jason loved Death Valley. He said the valley had one of the great unappreciated natural resources—silence. I remember Pahrump because the name looked so strange on the road sign. It's about sixty-five miles from Vegas, but only about twenty miles from Jason's cabin. Is that where the corporation is? Nevada Mining and whatever?"

"Nevada Mining and Assay. Yes, that's where it is."

"And that's who's after our property?"

"I think so, Barbara. I'll find out for sure tonight."

"Oh, James, you're not going out there by yourself, are you?"

"What do you think, Barbara?"

She started to speak, then seemed to reconsider. "I think I would be better off not asking."

"I think so too, woman."

As Hawker walked past her toward the door, she reached out and took his hand, then stood on tiptoe to kiss him tenderly on the lips. "Last night you promised you would come back. I want you to make the same promise tonight, James."

"I may be late, Barbara. Very late."

"Promise. Please."

In the light from the table lamp, her eyes looked like dark pools, and her hair was an ebony sheen. "If you like, Barbara. I promise. But don't wait up."

As Hawker reached for the door, he remembered something. "Barbara, last night—or very early this morning—someone visited me while I was asleep in your massage room. A woman. Did you send one of your girls?"

She shook her head. "No, James. You asked me not to."

"Was it you, Barbara?"

Her eyes did not change. "I was tempted, James. Very, very damn tempted."

"Is that an answer?"

"No."

"Why not?"

"Maybe it's because I'm a little envious. But you didn't strike me as the type of man who would settle for sleeping with someone he didn't care about."

"She caught me at a weak moment."

"Was it enjoyable?"

"The question is indiscreet. And the answer is yes. And underline the *yes*."

"Then I *am* envious. And you have all the more reason to hurry back in good health, James. Your mystery woman may be waiting for you."

FIFTEEN

Hawker drove west toward the sunset.

It was one of those spectacular desert sunsets. The sky was aflame with iridescent light. Orange rays fanned over a lavender horizon, with stormbursts of clouds backlighted in pink. The clouds were layered like desert buttes, peaking into smoky cobalt explosions of thunderheads.

It looked like a desert world above a desert land.

Hawker drove carefully. He had loaded the car with ordnance from his armaments supply. He couldn't risk being stopped for speeding. Even the most haphazard search would make an honest trooper's eyes bulge.

He had worked too hard to have it all ruined by a trip to some county jail now.

Hawker also kept his eyes open for any kind of tail. If they tried it again, he wouldn't waste time with any *Smoky and the Bandit* chase. It was too dangerous. And too time-consuming.

No, if they came after him now, he would simply pull over and fight it out.

And with the firepower he carried, it would take the National Guard to take him.

A very well-trained National Guard.

Hawker drove with the top down. He wore no suit jacket and tailored slacks now. At his apartment, he had changed into glove-soft jeans, running shoes, a black cotton woven sweater and a Navy issue watch cap.

The Randall was strapped to his calf, and the Smith & Wesson stainless steel .44 magnum he had selected as a handgun was in the custom-built shoulder holster with the spring-retention system. As an added precaution, he carried the little Walther PPK in the DFB ankle holster hidden beneath his jeans.

He would carry other weaponry, of course.

But these were the necessities. Hawker's own brand of life insurance.

Route 160 began to veer north. The mountains were off to his right, a masked darkness in the descending night. The village of Pahrump, he knew, lay ahead. And ten miles east of that, toward the Spring Mountains, was the Nevada Mining and Assay plant.

In the road wind was the delicate acidity of cactus and rank sand. The heat accumulated during the Nevada day boiled off the asphalt, but the desert breeze was dry and cool.

Hawker felt good. Finally this mission had come into sharp focus. After stopping at his suite, Hawker had taken the added precaution of taking the envelopes of rock samples he had found in Stratton's cabin to a Vegas lapidarist. The lapidarist had found most of the samples to be uninteresting.

But a conglomerate crystal glob, heavier than lead and the

color of wet tar, had caused him to do a double take. Then a triple take.

It was, indeed, pitchblende.

That was when Hawker knew beyond any shadow of a doubt that Nevada Mining and Assay was behind the brutal attacks on the people associated with the Five-Cs.

Hawker had prodded him for more information about pitchblende. When Hawker was satisfied with the answers, he began to ask questions only a local resident could answer. All the lapidarist could tell him was that Nevada Mining and Assay was a major industrial company that dealt in the processing of precious metal. The lapidarist also told him he had heard there was money from the Middle East involved. But that wasn't uncommon. American business was the favorite investment of Islamic oil money.

Even so, Hawker found it troubling. He tried to telephone Chief Smith to ask if the concern might be one of the "legitimate" businesses controlled by the mob.

For some reason, it would all seem a lot easier if the mob was behind it all.

But Chief Smith was under sedation, soon to enter surgery to have a bullet removed.

So Hawker headed for the western border of Nevada not knowing exactly who his enemy was. Or how prepared they would be to retaliate. All he did know was that they were merciless. And would stop at nothing.

Which was exactly why Hawker now traveled heavily armed.

Pahrump was little more than a collection of houses at an intersection of desert roads. Hawker turned east, toward the mountains.

The lights of the Jaguar bored through the summer darkness. When the road began its serpentine climb toward the mountains, Hawker hit the toggle switch, and the amber halogen fog lamps flooded the narrow road with light.

It crossed his mind that they might have guards watching the road. He kept a sharp eye as he drove, but saw nothing. There was only the wind sculpture of desert mesas and the softer darkness of mountains.

Nevada Mining and Assay Corporation came into view as Hawker topped an ascending series of small hills.

It lay in a valley, a sizable industrial complex enclosed by high chain link fence and illuminated by orange vapor lights. The main building was a corrugated steel structure, four stories high, with two levels of ore elevators angling up its side.

A railroad dump track led from the valley into the complex. Three empty cars sat within the compound. The track was sealed by a massive gate on the southern edge.

Beyond the tracks was an imposing white structure. It was built of cement, two stories high. There was a grim sterility about it, and Hawker guessed it was some kind of laboratory.

There were a few smaller outbuildings in the complex. They looked like they might be office huts and dormitories. At the far and near edge of the area were lighted guard towers. They gave the place a concentration camp flavor. Hawker decided the entire place covered about fifteen acres.

A long asphalt driveway descended to the complex from the main road.

Hawker slowed slightly as he passed the turnoff. The sign at the intersection was brightly lighted:

VEGAS VENGEANCE

Nevada Mining and Assay
An Investment in America
Absolutely No Entrance without Credentials
Trespassers will be prosecuted

Friendly place.

Hawker wondered just how they prosecuted trespassers. It reminded him of a sign he had seen once in the window of a college fraternity house:

No girls allowed. Trespassers will be violated.

A funny threat.

But there was nothing funny about the appearance of Nevada Mining and Assay.

The place had the look of one of those industrial concerns that did top-secret government work. Complex armament man-ufacture; precious metals; high tolerance machinery. Built far away from the mainstream industrial areas for a reason. All very hush-hush and low profile. And very damn deadly-looking.

If his observation was accurate, Hawker wondered just what government was underwriting the operation.

Not the people of United States, he hoped.

Hawker drove on past, the lights of the Jag tunneling through the darkness.

The air was cooler here, fresh out of the high mountains. Moths and insects veered toward his driving lights, flaming like comets. Hawker took a deep breath as he went over his plan.

An innocent plan, really.

First, he wanted to get evidence against the company. Jason Stratton had mentioned Nevada Mining and Assay in each of the last entries in his journal. Stratton had found the pitchblende but didn't have the instruments to gauge the extent of his find. So he took samples to their labs. In the June 10 entry, Stratton questioned their findings. He thought them inaccurate. It puzzled him. Anyone less innocent would have suspected the company's principals of trying to keep the discovery for themselves.

But not Jason Stratton.

Stratton's last entry mentioned he had questioned the findings by telephone, then had agreed to a meeting with officials from the mining company. The officials had insisted they couldn't make a proper analysis of the pitchblende without testing the area from which it came.

Stratton fell for it. He wrote how delighted he was that they took such pride in their work.

Jason Stratton would never make another entry.

A mile up the mountain road, Hawker turned off onto a gravel jeep trail. He backed the Jag into the brush in case he had to get away quickly.

From the glove compartment he took a little tin of military greasepaint and dabbed it on his face.

He checked the effect in the rearview mirror.

Satisfied, he opened the tiny trunk and chose the equipment he would carry. Since the first priority was getting into the complex, Hawker selected gear a burglar might need. He tried to anticipate every problem and choose the proper tool. If he could get into the file area, he wanted to be able to record any entries referring to Jason Stratton, so he decided to carry the tiny half-inch-frame camera. It was about the size of a pocketknife. He packed the gear carefully into a khaki knapsack. Then he turned his attention to weaponry.

Because he was in a mountainous area, he wanted to travel as light as possible. It's tough to run up a hill with eighty pounds of gear on your back. But he also wanted enough firepower to handle any situation.

For a shoulder gun, Hawker chose the Colt Commando automatic. The Colt was really a cut-down version of the M-16. It had been developed during Vietnam, where a tough, big firepower weapon was needed that could be used in extremely close quarters. The barrel had been shortened and a flash eliminator added. There was also a telescoping stock that, when stored, made the weapon less than thirty inches long.

The Colt fired standard 5.56-millimeter ammunition from twenty-round clips. On full automatic, it fired up to eight hundred rounds per minute—if you could feed it that fast.

Hawker had already preloaded ten clips, plus the one in the weapon.

He stored the clips in the knapsack and held them fast with a Velcro strap.

Fixed atop the Colt was the Star-Tron MK 303a night-vision system. It looked like an expensive telephoto camera lens. The Star-Tron's complex mirror system sucked in all available light—light from stars, the moon—then amplified it fifty thousand times. The resulting image through the scope was sharp and clear and as bright as high noon on a cloudy day.

Hawker switched on the Star-Tron, testing it. He turned the

weapon toward the dark mountain, and suddenly it was daylight. It was like looking at each individual tree through a glowing red filter.

Hawker switched off the scope and returned to the business of arming himself.

He took all the explosives he thought he might need—and others he hoped he wouldn't need.

Thinking there was an outside chance he could use it, Hawker had put a free-flight disposable missile launcher into the Jag. It was the M-72, manufactured by the United States Army. The M-72 was a telescoping tube that fired the extremely powerful 66-millimeter HEAT missile. Even fully armed, launcher and missile weighed less than five pounds. And there was a shoulder strap so it could be easily carried.

Hawker hesitated, then whispered, "What the hell."

After checking his equipment a final time, he urinated into the bushes, then picked up the Colt Commando, threw the rocket launcher over his shoulder and headed down the mountain toward the Nevada Mining and Assay stronghold.

SIXTEEN

Hawker had no illusions about the security system of the mining corporation. He knew it would be tough to get in undetected.

But it never crossed his mind that it might be impossible.

It nearly was.

He left the road and traveled cross-country. He kept low, sticking to the heavy tree cover on the hillside. Hawker knew that if the corporation was serious about keeping intruders out, it might equip its guards with the same state-of-the-art night-vision systems that he carried.

When he got close enough to check through the Star-Tron, he found out he was right.

There were two guards in each tower. Their night-vision systems were mounted on unipods. The guards took turns at the huge binoculars while the others manned what looked to be 50-caliber machine guns. The machine guns were positioned on mobile tripods, no doubt for daylight concealment.

But there was something else about the guards that Hawker found even more disconcerting. They were dressed in uniforms unfamiliar to Hawker. Their jackets had the pleats and drawn blouses usually associated with British officers. But these guards weren't British. They wore white turbans instead of field caps. And they certainly weren't Gurkhas.

It stunned Hawker momentarily. He could make no sense of it.

But then he remembered what the lapidarist had said about the rumor that Nevada Mining and Assay was controlled by Middle Eastern money. Money from the Islamic nations. Iraq or Saudi Arabia, Kuwait or Iran, or one of the other oil nations.

Suddenly all the little pieces fell neatly into place. And the picture the completed puzzle made was frightening as hell.

How could such a thing happen in a country as powerful as the United States? But then, without another moment's thought, Hawker knew. America was controlled by a Congress that was all too soft on outsiders who wanted in; a Congress that insisted the laws of business acquisition be applied to aliens with the same free hand that was extended to Americans. They had, in effect, opened the doors of the vault and ushered the enemies in, bidding them to sit down, relax and take what they wanted.

This was the Congress of the limousine liberals. Rich kids disguised as adult intellectuals. Men and women with egos proportional to their families' wealth, who sneeringly dismissed the middle-class conservatives as Archie Bunker clones. And just as all spoiled children one day turn against their parents, these "public servants" had turned against the source of their parents' wealth—America. These were the destructive ones. They shielded themselves with humanitarian banners while methodically trying to break the backs of the middle class with their welfare states and open-door policies.

Hawker could not stomach them.

But now they had opened the door too far. If what Hawker suspected was true, even the liberals of the Democratic far left could not ignore this threat.

Or perhaps they could. Perhaps they would welcome it.

Hawker slowly lowered the Star-Tron scope. It crossed his mind that what he had uncovered was a danger of such great magnitude that he should perhaps contact federal authorities. Get help. Because, after all, there was the possibility that he might fail.

But what would he tell them? That he had seen guards wearing turbans?

They would laugh him right out the door.

No, he needed proof. Then and only then could he risk bringing in the authorities.

Hawker sat in the darkness for a long minute, thinking. When he was confident that what he was about to do was right, he moved off quickly toward the complex.

There was a twenty-yard killing area between the fence and the tree line. Hawker stopped just within the tree line, about a hundred yards from the front gate. The chain link fence, he noticed, wasn't constructed of standard galvanized steel. It seemed to be made of a darker, glossier metal, as were the strands of barbed wire atop it.

It could mean only one thing: the fence was electrified.

Once again, Hawker looked through the Star-Tron scope, checking to see if anything extended over the fence—a tree limb, a telephone drop line, anything he could use to cross.

There was nothing.

It gave him only two options. The first option left a lot to luck: he could wait and hope a delivery truck or some such came down the road, then sneak a ride on it.

Hawker settled on the second option.

He made his way back up the hillside to the main road. He followed the power lines to one of the secondary transformers. It was no easy job shimmying up the pole and planting the small charge of plastic explosives, but he managed.

He was still sweating by the time he got back to the tree line outside the complex. The mining company would have a generator override system, of course. But Hawker was betting he could get through the fence before the generator kicked in.

He pulled on a pair of black leather gloves and laid out the heavy wire cutters before aiming the electronic detonator in the direction of the transformer. He hit the toggle switch.

The explosion was small: a sharp *whoof* and a shower of sparks in the distance. He had heard much louder transformer explosions, and was sure this one would cause no undue concern inside the complex.

The moment the lights on the guard towers flickered and went out, Hawker sprinted toward the fence, cut a vertical slash in it and crawled through.

The darkness, he knew, wouldn't last long. Once he got to his feet, he ran toward the closest building—a corrugated toolshed—and dove behind it.

A second later, there was a generator whir, the vapor lights glowed, and soon the complex was brightly lighted again.

The blackout, though, had brought the camp to life. Voices

called to each other from unseen sources. Doors opened and slammed shut. Dark figures moved into the open area beneath the guard tower. Many of them wore turbans. All looked to be East Indian. The man obviously in charge wore a neatly tailored officer's uniform, the jacket unbuttoned as if he had been roused from an easy chair.

Hawker could not see him clearly. And he could not understand the language they spoke. But he did hear the man's name spoken once, voiced loudly as one of the guards called for him.

His name was Hamadan.

Hawker knew he would have to wait until things settled down. To move now would be to commit suicide.

It was 10:18 according to his Seiko Submariner.

He flattened himself against the ground and carefully planned his course of action as he waited. To his left were the guard tower and the main gate. Ahead of him was the four-story steel building. Behind that was the imposing cement structure.

Hawker decided he would break into the concrete building first. It looked like a laboratory, and the laboratory was probably where they would have records of their dealings with Jason Stratton.

By 11:10, it was sufficiently quiet to move.

Hawker crawled on elbows and knees across the clearing, aware that at any second, one of the guards could open fire. The small outbuildings were the only cover he had, and he used them. Once he passed so close to a dormitory that he could hear the men laughing and talking through the open windows.

When he finally arrived at the cement building, the nerve-racking work began. The painstaking work of careful burglary. From his knapsack, Hawker took two vials. One was an extremely powerful but inert acid. The other was the catalyst that would activate the acid. Using an eyedropper, Hawker deposited drops in both locks of the steel door. The acid fumed and hissed, eating away the internal works.

When that was done, Hawker took a long wire with alligator clips on both ends. The burglar alarm, he hoped, would be standard in that the door would be wired to an internal electrical circuit. Any break in the circuit would set off the alarm.

Hawker cracked the door just enough to see the conductor plates on the door and door seal. He hooked an alligator clip to each conductor plate, then opened the door enough for him to slide through—and was damn careful not to kick the wire loose as he did.

Once the door was closed behind him, Hawker breathed easier.

The hallway of the building was dark. The floor was cold linoleum. The place had an astringent odor, a mixture of alcohol and industrial-strength cleaner.

Hawker went quickly down the hall, peering into the rooms. It was, indeed, a laboratory. The place was filled with complex-looking electronic equipment and rooms with long marble tables.

He knew there had to be some kind of office center, and he finally found it. A wide, efficient room with modern desks, personal computers and typewriters. An unfamiliar flag was draped on a pole in the corner. Hawker took the time to unfurl it: red, white and blue horizontal bands. In the center were three green stars.

It took Hawker a moment to place it.

It was the flag of Iraq. The country of the lunatic dictator and his lunatic followers.

One of their jets had once attacked a Navy Phantom. And the Iraqi had been blown into the wild blue yonder.

Hawker released the flag. Sweat beaded on his forehead. The bastards were really doing it. They were really going to try it right under America's nose.

Hawker moved quickly now. The file cabinets were locked, but it was an easy matter to lift them and extract the lock bar from beneath. But that did not help. All the files were in Arabic.

Frustrated, Hawker turned to the computers on the desks. Their keyboards were locked, and there were no keys to be seen. But then he realized something that he found astounding. As evidenced by the disc drives, the computers weren't hooked in to a main computer bank. All their information was kept on 5½-inch floppy disks—and the disks were stored in ready view in plastic files atop the desks. The stupidity of such a thing in a compound protected by such a complex security system almost made him laugh.

But he didn't take the time to laugh. He cracked open the plastic files and began packing the disks into his knapsack.

When he had them all, he hurried through the doorway and back down the hall so that he might retrace his steps to the mountainside and freedom.

But it wasn't to be.

As he passed one of the hallway intersections, a dark figure jumped out at him. The figure had something in its hand. Something dark and heavy and very, very hard.

And then the world went all dreamy and star bright, and James Hawker was falling, falling, fighting to stay in the world of the conscious . . . and the world of the living.

SEVENTEEN

Hawker battled the unconsciousness, fought the withering pain as he went down.

He knew that to fall unconscious was to die.

And the stakes were much too high for that. The stakes were far more important than his own life.

As Hawker tumbled downward, his right hand swept toward the shoulder holster that held the Smith & Wesson .44 magnum. The weight of it was cool and solid in his fist.

His attacker was a bulky dark shadow to the left, stooped from having just delivered the blow. There was something in his hand. A club, maybe. Or perhaps the butt of a revolver.

Hawker hit the floor with his shoulder and rolled. The attacker's boot slammed the floor behind him, trying to smash Hawker's head.

The vigilante squeezed off two quick shots. The .44 magnum sounded like a cannon. The explosions rang down the hallway, and there was the good smell of gunpowder.

His attacker was catapulted backward against the wall. The

sound of bone and flesh cracking against cement was sickening. It was as if he had been hit by a speeding truck.

But the man never felt the impact of collision.

The powerful .44 slugs had ripped his chest apart. He was dead before he ever hit the ground.

Hawker got woozily to his knees. He touched his head and wondered why he was sweating so badly. He studied the black sheen on his hands stupidly. It took him a long moment to realize he wasn't sweating. He was bleeding.

He sat heavily on the floor, fighting the urge to lie down and rest for a moment. He had been in that gauzy, slow-motion world of near-unconsciousness before. Back in his boxing days. And he knew that if he held on, the worst of it would pass.

He sat and waited. After the two gunshots, he expected to hear the alarms and gongs and sirens of warning. He expected lights to flash on as the Iraqi soldiers came running to kill him.

But there was only silence.

Maybe the laboratory was better insulated than most buildings. Maybe the sound of the gunshots had not passed through the thick cement walls.

Hawker didn't want to wait around too long to find out.

To his right was a door on which was posted the silhouette of a man wearing a hat.

A restroom.

Hawker got shakily to his feet, pushed through the doorway and switched on the light.

An eerie stranger looked back at him from the mirror. The left side of his face was covered with blood. Beneath the blood was the khaki greasepaint. It made him look like some jungle creature who had snuck to a water hole after devouring its fresh kill.

Hawker took off the Navy watch cap and inspected his wound. It wasn't as bad as he'd thought. The skin had split like a ripe plum, but the skull was still firm. If it hadn't been for the cushion of his wool cap, the blow might have killed him.

He rinsed his head under cold water until the bleeding slowed, then went back out into the hall.

All was still quiet. The corpse lay sprawled on the floor in a lake of blood.

Hawker's mission had been accomplished for the night. He had stolen the computer records undetected, and now all he had to do was make his escape.

So why was he so reluctant to leave?

He knew. Getting in had been relatively easy. Getting out was another matter. The fence was still electrified, and there was no way he could futz the power lines from within. That meant he would have to blast his way out. And that would bring him a lot of attention. Deadly attention.

There was the very real chance he wouldn't be able to outrun them. Maybe Wendy Nierson, the free mountain spirit, was right. Maybe he would die very soon.

Maybe he would die tonight.

If so, Hawker was damn determined to take "Iraqi" Mining and Assay and most of its men with him.

Pulling a blue sausage roll of plastic explosives from his knapsack, Hawker began molding heavy charges to the foundation of the building and to the complex electronic apparatus in the lab.

Into each charge he inserted an electronic detonating device.

It was just after midnight when he finished. He made his way back to the front door and crawled outside, once again being careful not to trip his own extension wire.

The compound was quiet. The guards in their towers surveyed the tree line beyond the fence, obviously confident that they need fear attack only from the outside. Shortly, Hawker knew, they would discover just how wrong they were. Because soon he would have to blast his way out and run for his life.

Hawker's eyes settled on the massive corrugated ore processing plant fifty meters away. Until it came time to run, he might as well do all the damage he could.

He crawled on elbows and knees to the wall of the factory. Flush against the back wall were two massive steel pods built on stilts: chemical storage units.

The vigilante planted heavy charges beneath each of them and inserted the detonators. He would have liked to get inside the factory and plant charges there, but he would have had to go through the time-consuming burglary ritual again.

Besides, when the chemical tanks went, half the ore processing plant would go with them.

Satisfied with his work, Hawker began to consider through which portion of the fence he should try to escape. It seemed unwise to return the way he had come, for that would put his pursuers on a beeline course to the Jaguar.

Hawker had just settled on using one of his grenades to blow open the gate at the railroad dump track when he noticed the silhouette of a man against the window of one of the smaller outbuildings.

There was something familiar in the man's face structure and carriage; something in the unbuttoned officer's jacket that touched one of the memory electrodes.

Then Hawker knew. He had seen him earlier. Just after the lights came back on. It was the man who had shouted out orders in Arabic. It was the man they called Hamadan.

Hawker couldn't resist the opportunity.

He put the grenade away and crawled to the cottage. He stood and stole a look through the window. It was, indeed, Hamadan. He sat in a chair, with his feet on an ottoman. There was a drink on the table beside him, and there were papers and charts in his lap.

Hawker had seen his silhouette when he'd gotten up to get the drink.

The vigilante went to the door and tapped twice.

Hamadan called out something in Arabic.

Hawker tapped again.

The moment the door opened, Hawker jammed the barrel of the Smith & Wesson .44 into the Iraqi's face and forced his way in. He closed the door quietly behind.

"What do you think you are doing!" Hamadan blurted, instantly regretting that he had spoken in English.

Hawker smiled. "That's just what I wanted to hear, Hamadan. I need some answers, and I had a feeling you were the man who could give them to me. I came here to look for a friend of mine. A guy named Jason Stratton."

"Stratton? I know no one named Stratton. Now please, let go of my hair and take that gun from my face—"

Hawker pulled back the hammer of the Smith & Wesson. "I

know too much for you to lie to me, Hamadan. Remember that. Because the next time you lie, I'm going to pull this trigger. No more warnings, no more second chances. Just bang, and you're bound for a closed casket funeral." Hawker yanked the man's head roughly. "Now talk!"

Hamadan had the olive complexion and carefully tended mustache common among his countrymen. But the whimper that escaped his lips suggested he lacked the zealot's courage. "Yes, yes, maybe I do remember that name," he said quickly. "A man named Stratton brought some minerals to us for testing. He said he lacked the proper equipment."

"He brought some samples of pitchblende, right?"

Hamadan's eyes grew more worried. The American obviously did know at least part of the story. "Yes," he said. "It was pitchblende. Mr. Stratton was very excited. He had found several samples in sedimentary clastic deposits in an ancient riverbed near Las Vegas. But he was uncertain if the pitchblende was of the uranite variety."

"And it was?"

Hamadan hesitated. "Yes. Yes, it was."

"Now," Hawker coached, "tell me why Stratton would find that so exciting. What's so special about the uranite variety of pitchblende?"

"I think you already know. So why is it you ask me—"

"Talk, damnit!" Hawker demanded in a hoarse whisper.

"Uranium. Uranium is processed from the uranite variety of pitchblende. To find a reliable source of pitchblende is a discovery greater than a gold mine, for it is far more valuable. Mr. Stratton was quite certain he had found such a source."

"And he showed you the source?"

Once again, the Iraqi hesitated. His eyes searched James Hawker's face to see if he might attempt a lie. It didn't take him long to decide. "Yes, Stratton took me there. A shallow valley where they had built a gambling complex and a house of prostitution. I thought it rather funny that the Americans had built their businesses on property that could produce more money for them in a month than their gambling casinos could produce in two years. My . . . my country, as you may know, is absolutely desperate for a reliable source of pitch blende. It is for that reason we founded this mining operation—to look for such a source. We have looked with only minor success for the entire five years of our existence. And then to have a stranger walk in from nowhere with a truly spectacular find—"

"So you murdered him. You murdered Jason Stratton and then tried to force the owners of the Five-Cs complex to sell. You hired American killers to do your dirty work so you would not be connected in any way."

The Iraqi dropped to his knees, his hands clasped as if in prayer. "You must understand that it was his life against the lives of thousands! Millions, even! My country has the same right to nuclear capabilities as the major powers! Allah has instructed our supreme leader in these matters. We must take our rightful place in this world; we must fulfill our destiny! But Stratton would not listen. He did not believe in us or trust us—"

"I wouldn't trust you goat suckers with a firecracker," Hawker snapped. A cold fury had built in him as he listened to the Iraqi beg. He backhanded Hamadan across the face, a blow that sent the Iraqi sliding across the floor with such velocity that he knocked the nightstand over. The telephone fell on top of him, and the Iraqi's eyes widened in slow realization. There were two red buttons on the phone, and the Iraqi punched both of them rapidly.

Outside, Hawker heard the wild wail of a siren. Hamadan had hit some kind of emergency alarm. Hawker turned to the front door and peered out the window. Soldiers were pouring out of the dormitories, dressing themselves as they ran. They were collecting around a small Israeli-built JL-14 armored riot car. The riot car had a fifty-caliber machine gun mounted on a turret, and the machine gun vectored toward Hamadan's quarters as the driver started the engine.

A noise behind him brought Hawker's head swinging around. Hamadan was on his feet. Somewhere he had found a gun. A tiny automatic. Found it in the drawer of the overturned table, perhaps.

The automatic popped loudly, and Hawker felt a dull stinging sensation in his left shoulder. He raised the Smith & Wesson .44 magnum and squeezed the trigger in rapid fire.

The Iraqi's face sprayed flesh as the right side of his head disappeared, the impact tumbling him backward onto the bed.

"Bad choice of weapons, asshole," Hawker hissed at the corpse.

Outside, they had heard the shots.

The roar of the armor-plated riot car was growing near.

Favoring his left side, Hawker unstrapped the M-72 free-flight missile launcher. He snapped off the protective caps at either end, then pulled out the inner tube and locked it into position. He flipped up the plastic reticle sights before sliding in the two-pound HEAT missile with its M-18 warhead.

When he was ready, Hawker kicked open the door and stood ready to take the Iraqis with him into the dark and bottomless abyss of death.

EIGHTEEN

Hawker pressed the trigger button.

There was a microsecond delay, then the HEAT missile *whooshed* in a serpentine trail of flame toward the armored riot car.

Fifteen or twenty Iraqi soldiers marched in disorder behind the small tank. They didn't even have time to react.

Traveling at 145 meters a second, the rocket blew the riot car high into the air through sheer impact. The explosion was deafening: a gas ball of orange flame ballooned into the darkness, illuminating the grisly spectacle of dead or dying soldiers on the ground.

Hawker dropped the disposable launcher on the floor, picked up the Colt Commando and sprinted outside.

The entire left side of his body ached now, and his black cotton sweater was soaked with blood. But there was no time to stop and take inventory. He knew the chaos wouldn't last long. If he was to escape, this was the time. And if he couldn't—then he would hit the electronic detonator in his pocket and take most of "Iraqi" Mining and Assay with him.

Forgetting that he shouldn't head straight for the hidden Jaguar, Hawker ran toward the section of fence where he had entered. In the knapsack was a TH3 incendiary grenade with which he planned to blow open the electrified fence.

But as he ran, the guards in the towers spotted him and opened up with their fifty-caliber machine guns. Dirt plumed up in front of him. Hawker skidded to a halt and dove behind an aluminum toolshed.

The fifty-caliber slugs tore through it as easily as if it were a beer can.

Hawker got to his feet and sprinted into the darkness. As he neared Hamadan's cottage, three soldiers jumped out in front of him. Holding the Colt Commando in one hand, Hawker pressed the trigger on full automatic. The soldiers crumpled and were catapulted into the air.

Behind him, the guards again opened up with their fifty-calibers. Hawker dove behind the hut just as the slugs began stripping off the aluminum siding. The vigilante took a moment to punch out the spent clip and slide a fresh one into the Commando. As he did, he drew out the incendiary grenade and forced it into his left hand—which now served as little more than a claw.

Ahead of him were the three railroad cars. They were open-bed cars, built to haul ore. Hawker took a deep breath, then ran just as hard as he could toward them. The fifty-caliber slugs clanked off the steel bed in front of him as his left foot found the switchman's bullard on the side of the car and he threw himself up into the empty car.

Hawker landed harder than he'd expected. It sent a nauseating wave of pain through his left shoulder.

Outside, he could hear voices shouting and heavy footsteps as the soldiers descended on his position.

From the towers, guards sprayed the railroad car so that Hawker could not stand and return fire. The heavy slugs made a deafening clatter as they ricocheted off the thick metal of the car.

It was then James Hawker realized there was no escape for him. This would be his tomb: a ruststained coffin built to haul earth, not flesh.

But he wasn't about to go without taking a few more with him.

Groggily Hawker sat up. The guards were closer now. He could hear their excited Arabic just outside as they decided who would be the first to risk climbing onto the car.

Hawker reached into his pocket and pulled out the electronic detonator. It was the size of a pocket computer, but with a telescoping antenna and two toggle switches.

Then he took the TH3 incendiary grenade from his left hand, pulled the pin with his teeth and lobbed the canister over the wall of the railroad car.

The grenade, armed with 750 grams of thermate, exploded with a searing flash of streaming white smoke rays. The thermate burned at more than two thousand degrees centigrade, and Hawker could feel the withering heat through the steel walls. The screams were hideous—but gratifying.

The grenade had bought him time.

Hawker pulled himself to his feet. The pain was agonizing, but he managed to point the detonator's antenna over the side of the railroad car, then flip both toggle switches.

It was like the end of the world.

The explosion of the chemical tanks threw a brilliant volcanic plume a thousand feet into the air as the ore processing plant and the laboratory thumped and screamed with scarlet flames in a series of smaller explosions.

The railroad car shook violently as if in an earthquake. Weak as he was, the earth's rumbling knocked Hawker off his feet, and he fell heavily on his back.

And still the railroad car vibrated and shook.

It took Hawker a long moment to realize that the car continued to shake because it was moving. Knocked free by the explosion, the car was rolling down the grade, picking up momentum. There was a grinding crash as it burst through the chain link fence. Hawker felt a slight shock. On generator power, apparently, the fence was no longer lethal. The car continued to roll, gaining speed.

Hawker settled back, too weary even to stand and see what lay ahead—or what followed.

He concentrated only on breathing deeply, gathering his remaining strength. Overhead, he could see tree limbs flashing past. They were dark and reassuring beneath the blaze of Nevada stars.

Even though it was really only five or six minutes, it seemed as if he traveled for a long time. Soon the car began to slow; then it stopped, then rolled backward for a short distance.

Hawker forced himself to get to his feet. He peered over the walls of the ore car. The railroad track was a shadowy path, empty in the distance.

The Iraqis had not followed.

Not yet, anyway.

Climbing out was not easy. Hawker got one leg over the edge but lost his balance when his right hand slipped and gave way. He fell in a heap onto the rocky base of the railroad bed.

He knew that inevitably the Iraqis would come for him.

He knew he had to move, had to use his precious last reserve of strength to get away.

So he crawled.

He crawled on his hands and knees into the mountain woods; crawled through the cool brush and the scent of earth musk, over rocks and stumps; crawled for a very long way until he could crawl no more.

Then he collapsed beneath a rock ledge, curled up in a fetal position, the Smith & Wesson .44 clasped in his right hand.

Hawker awoke just before sunrise. A pearly fog had settled on the mountainside, so it took him a moment to realize that a person stood over him, watching him.

He brought the .44 up to fire. But the revolver was gone. Someone had taken it.

He struggled to get to his feet, but his left arm refused to move.

Then the figure drew closer and touched his face gently. It was a woman. She wore a shirt and baggy jeans in the chilly morning air, and her blond hair hung down over her shoulders.

"James, James," she said softly, "you'll be all right now. You're badly hurt, but you're going to live."

It seemed as if the words were coming to him down a long tunnel, and it took what seemed a long time to place the voice.

It was the free spirit from Spring Mountain.

"Wendy?" Hawker croaked in a voice that did not sound like his own. "But how in the hell did you find me? How did you know where to look?"

She kissed him tenderly on the hand. "You called for me, James. All night, you called. I heard you in my dreams."

NINETEEN

Three weeks later, James Hawker returned to Las Vegas for the first time since his assault on the Iraqis.

Wendy Nierson and the rest of the Spring Mountain Family had nursed him back to health. They had reacted happily to his demand that they not take him to a hospital or notify the police.

The Spring Mountain Family had little respect for either.

But they did agree to call Kevin Smith and tell him where he was and that he would be all right.

So he lived with them, ate with them and became so used to their nudity that after the first week, Hawker also removed his clothes so he could limp around the camp without drawing undue attention.

At first, it was a strange feeling. But he soon grew to like it. Almost as much as he came to like Wendy Nierson.

Wendy was like no other woman Hawker had ever been with. Unlike most of the hippies he'd known back in the sixties, she was a true free spirit. She was tender and sentimental and full of enthusiasm and wild interests. Whenever Hawker asked for more details on how she had "heard him calling in her dreams," she only smiled mysteriously and changed the subject.

On the tenth night of his stay with the Spring Mountain Family, they became lovers. And he was gladdened to find that while Wendy Nierson might be a laid-back pacifist by day, she was an absolute tigress by night. After their first coupling, she told him firmly that she knew he would ultimately leave her; knew he was not a one-woman man; and, because she knew all these things, that he should feel no guilt when the day for his leaving came.

The woman could be such an enigma with her sly smiles and her gift for extrasensory perception that Hawker had, in those first days, wondered if she might be the mystery woman who had come to him that night in the Doll House.

The logistics troubled him. For one thing, how could she have made it through the tight security of the Doll House? But his suspicions were all laid to rest their first night in bed together.

Wendy Nierson was mysterious. But she was not the mystery woman. In bed, she was completely different from that unknown woman with the odd musk perfume.

It was a strange three weeks, living with the Spring Mountain Family. But a good three weeks. It was an alternative lifestyle that Hawker would have scoffed at in earlier times. So he was surprised at how attractive he found it. Home-grown food. Honest talk. Discussion about subjects Hawker had barely considered before.

The Spring Mountain Family, of course, had no televisions or radios, so Hawker was honestly touched when Wendy one day surprised him by appearing in camp with an armful of Las

Vegas newspapers. It was through them that he anxiously traced the follow-up stories on the Iraqi mining camp.

According to the papers, the Iraqis had plotted to mine their own uranium and ship it out of the country to Iraq, where a nuclear reactor was already under construction.

Somehow, according to the newspaper, an American vigilante group had found out. They attacked and destroyed the camp. According to the few Iraqi survivors, it was a vigilante army of twenty or thirty Americans.

News of the battle brought in the FBI, and now the whole incident was under investigation. Proving to be of great help to the FBI's investigation were the alien group's records, which had been sent to Washington by an anonymous source, presumably the American vigilante group.

Nevada Mining and Assay, of course, no longer existed.

Congressional liberals raised a great hue and cry over such outrageous right wing behavior. They placed a motion before their fellows calling for a public apology to Iraq.

The motion, of course, passed.

Hawker thought about all these things as he maneuvered the Jaguar down the mountain road into Las Vegas, then turned up the drive to the Doll House. Barbara Blaine had tried to visit him twice during his stay on the mountain. The first time he was still unconscious and could not see her. The second time he was out hiking with Wendy, so he missed her again.

So now he came for both a reunion and a farewell. He was going back to Chicago because he didn't want to be around when the FBI investigation hit full stride.

Besides, his work in Las Vegas was done.

Barbara Blaine was in her suite when Hawker arrived. She wore white slacks and a pale orange blouse, and her ebony hair was braided and hung to the middle of her back. When she saw Hawker at the door, she trotted toward him with her arms thrown out.

"It's about damn time you came to see me!" She looked up at him with misty eyes, then drew back quickly when she noticed how he winced and favored his left side. "You're still hurt, James. Maybe you shouldn't be up!"

Hawker smiled and gave her a quick kiss on the cheek. "I'm fine. Just a little sore. But that'll be gone soon."

"You can stay for a while?"

"Awhile. I have a plane to catch in the morning."

"So we can talk over lunch?"

"If the lunch comes to us, we can talk all you want."

The woman ordered food while Hawker found himself a cold Tuborg in the refrigerator—his first beer since going to the mountain. And then they sat on the patio and Hawker gave her an edited version of what had happened in the Iraqi camp, taking special care to leave out the horror of it; the sounds, the smells, the screams and the acid stink of his own perspiring fear.

Then it was the woman's turn. She told about reading Jason Stratton's journal. She described the shock of learning that the Five-Cs was built over a massive deposit of pitchblende. Then she told him about something that surprised even Hawker.

"They found Jason two days ago," she said in a small voice.

"They?"

"The FBI. It was in the papers. They found him in a mine

shaft not far from Nevada Mining and Assay. He was still in his jeep. They had sealed the shaft with rocks. He had been shot."

"I'm sorry, Barbara."

"Reading his journal . . . it was like talking to him again. It reminded me of how very valuable he was. And how much I loved him." She looked up at Hawker suddenly. "I think Jason was my one chance at a normal life, Hawk, a life of husband and kids and a house in the country. Does that seem like a tragic thing to say?"

"No. But you're still in mourning, Barbara. Don't give up on your life yet. You may feel differently a year from now."

She shook her head. "Maybe I will, James. But you know something of my past. I don't meet many men that I find interesting. And that's why I've decided to keep the Doll House as it is. I had to do a little research as I read Jason's journal. I found out about pitchblende, so I know just how valuable it is. I suppose I could be a millionaire many times over if I chose to have this property mined. But where would my girls go? What would I do?" She smiled at him as her brown eyes filled. "I have a chance to do some real good here; a chance to help women make their own way in the world. And that's exactly what I've decided to do. And, James?"

"Yes, Barbara?"

"If you would like to stay here for a while . . . a few weeks or even longer, I'd be happy to have you. Not as a lover, but as a friend. The girls like you. I like you. It would be a comfort to us all having you around. No one would even have to know. And from the looks of you, a little more time to recuperate wouldn't hurt."

Hawker was about to give a polite refusal but was interrupted when the door to Barbara Blaine's suite opened and in stepped Mary Kay O'Mordecai Flynn. She was dazzling in a white jumpsuit. Her red hair was combed long, and her green eyes flashed when she saw Hawker.

"Mr. Hawker, I wondered what happened to you!" Then, slightly embarrassed, she turned quickly to Barbara Blaine. "Oh, if I'm interrupting, Barb, I'll—"

"No, no, come on in, Mary Kay. I was just trying to talk James into staying with us for a few weeks."

"Oh, that would be great, Mr. Hawker! It would be nice to have a man around for a change." When Mary Kay realized what a revealing thing that was to say about a house of prostitution, she covered her mouth with her hand and began laughing.

Then Barbara Blaine began to laugh, a full-throated gust, like a much-needed release.

But Hawker wasn't laughing. For the first time he noticed that Mary Kay wasn't alone. Behind her stood a woman who possessed an even more spectacular beauty. Her hair was also a tawny auburn; her legs long and tanned in their white short shorts; her face perfect with full lips and high cheeks and bright blue eyes.

It was a woman he had seen before. It was the woman he had watched at the pool outside his veranda at the Five-Cs.

When Mary Kay saw what he was looking at, she got control of herself and said, still giggling, "Mr. Hawker, I don't think you've met my sister, Kelly. Or, I should say, Dr. Kelly O'Mordecai Flynn. Kelly's on sabbatical. She's been staying at the house with me."

Before Hawker could speak, Kelly O'Mordecai Flynn was

walking toward him, her hand outstretched. There was a wry smile on her face, and Hawker caught a whiff of musky perfume that he recognized from that night in the massage room. "But we *have* already met, Mary Kay," Kelly O'Mordecai Flynn said in a Bacall-like voice, winking ever so slightly. "Haven't we, Mr. Hawker?"

Hawker looked deeply into the vixen eyes and returned the inviting squeeze of her hand. "Never formally, Dr. Flynn. But since I'm going to be staying here for a few weeks, I guess it was just a matter of time."

ABOUT THE AUTHOR

Randy Wayne White was born in Ashland, Ohio, in 1950. Best known for his series featuring retired NSA agent Doc Ford, he has published over twenty crime fiction and nonfiction adventure books. White began writing while working as a fishing guide in Florida, where most of his books are set. His earlier writings include the Hawker series, which he published under the pen name Carl Ramm. White has received several awards for his fiction, and his novels have been featured on the *New York Times* bestseller list. He was a monthly columnist for *Outside* magazine and has contributed to several other publications, as well as lectured throughout the United States and travelled extensively. White currently lives on Pine Island in South Florida, and remains an active member of the community through his involvement with local civic affairs as well as the restaurant Doc Ford's Sanibel Rum Bar and Grill.

HAWKER EBOOKS

OPEN ROAD

INTEGRATED MEDIA

Open Road Integrated Media is a digital publisher and multimedia content company. Open Road creates connections between authors and their audiences by marketing its ebooks through a new proprietary online platform, which uses premium video content and social media.

Videos, Archival Documents, and New Releases

Sign up for the Open Road Media newsletter and get news delivered straight to your inbox.

Sign up now at
www.openroadmedia.com/newsletters

FIND OUT MORE AT
WWW.OPENROADMEDIA.COM

FOLLOW US:
@openroadmedia and
Facebook.com/OpenRoadMedia

Westminster Public Library
3705 W. 112th Ave.
Westminster, CO 80031
www.westminsterlibrary.org

CPSIA information can be obtained at www.ICGtesting.com
Printed in the USA
LVOW11s1819080416

482782LV00001B/26/P